Kiran Millwood
Hargrave

The GIRL of INK & STARS

Chicken House

2 Palmer Street, Frome, Somerset BA11 1DS
chickenhousebooks.com

Text © Kiran Millwood Hargrave 2016

First published in Great Britain in 2016
Chicken House
2 Palmer Street
Frome, Somerset BA11 1DS
United Kingdom
www.chickenhousebooks.com

Cover and interior design by Helen Crawford-White
Cover illustration: silhouette, adapted from a photo by Buffy Cooper/
Trevillion Images; waves © Miloje/Shutterstock
Inside illustrations: compasses © Vertyr/Shutterstock;
ships/sea creatures/map icons © pavila/Shutterstock
Typeset by Dorchester Typesetting Group Ltd
Printed and bound in Great Britain by CPI Group (UK) Ltd, Croydon CR0 4YY

The paper used in this Chicken House book is made from
wood grown in sustainable forests.

17

British Library Cataloguing in Publication data available.

PB ISBN 978-1-910002-74-2
eISBN 978-1-910655-58-0

For a star, Sabine Karer
at 28.6139° N, 77.2090° E

and for those who helped me put ink to paper
at 51.7519° N, 1.2578° W

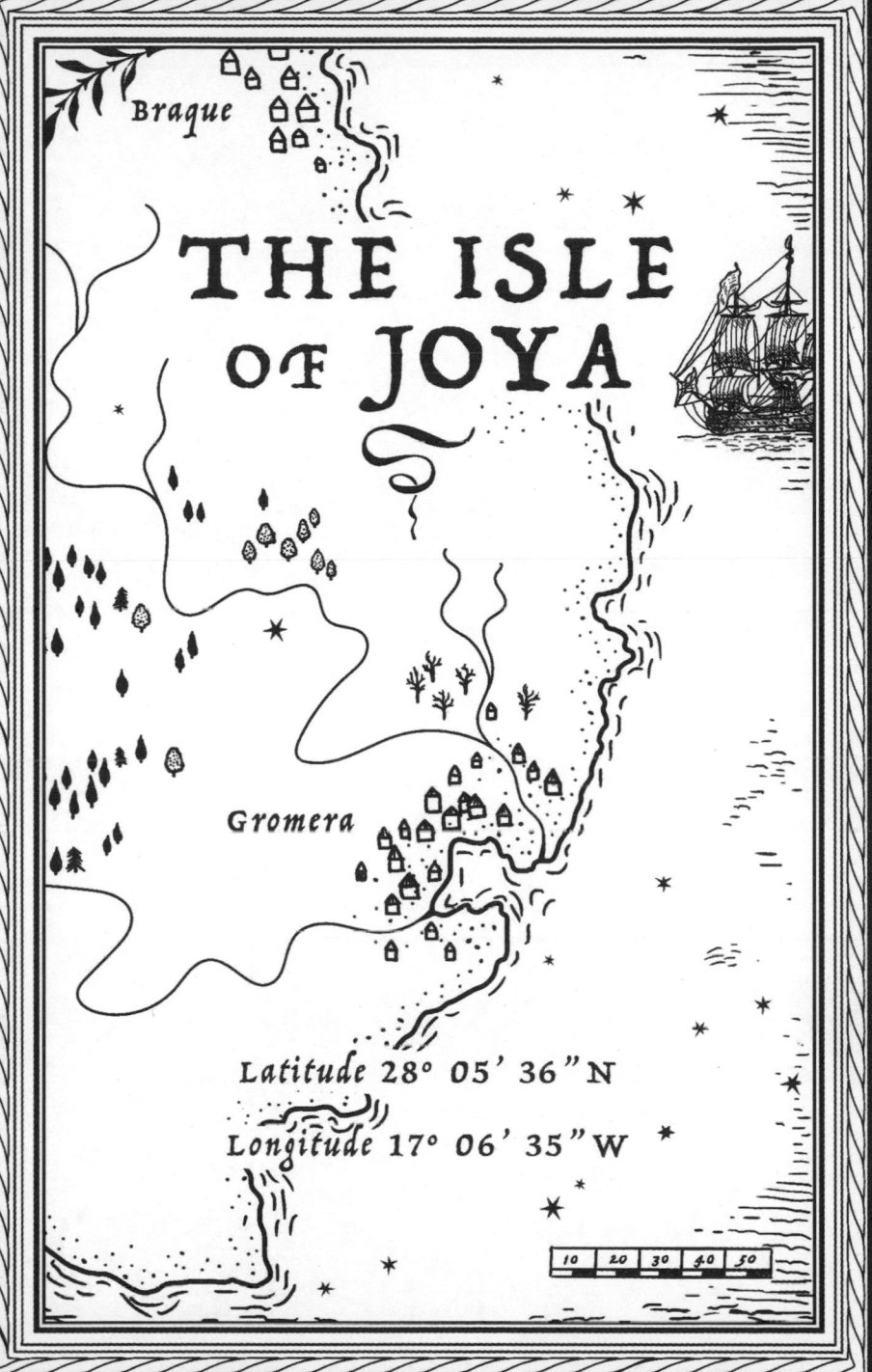

THE ISLE OF JOYA

Braque

Gromera

Latitude 28° 05' 36" N

Longitude 17° 06' 35" W

CHAPTER
ONE

They say the day the Governor arrived, the ravens did too. All the smaller birds flew backwards into the sea, and that is why there are no songbirds on Joya. Only huge, ragged ravens. I'd watch them perch on the rooftops like omens, and try to squint them into the chaffinches and goldcrests Da drew from memory. If I imagined hard enough, I could almost hear them singing.

'Why did the songbirds leave, Da?' I'd ask.

'Because they could, Isabella.'

'And the wolves? The deer?'

Da's face would darken. 'Seems the sea was better than what they were running from.'

Da would tell me another story then, about the girl-warrior Arinta, or about Joya's mythical past as a floating island, and refuse to say more about the wolves and the backwards birds. But I kept asking, until the day came when

I found my own answers.

The morning it began was like any other.

I woke in my narrow bed, sunrise just starting to brighten the mud walls of my room. The smell of burnt porridge hung on the air. Da must have been up for hours, as it took a long time for the fire to heat the heavy clay pot. I could hear Miss La, our hen, scratching about outside my room, seeking out crumbs. She was thirteen years old, same as me, but even though it's young for a person, it's very, very old for a chicken. Her feathers were grey, her mood was black and even our cat Pep was scared of her.

My tummy rumbled as I stretched my arms. Pep was sprawled across my legs, and he yowled loudly as I sat up.

'You awake, Isabella?' Da called from the kitchen.

'Morning, Da.'

'Porridge is ready. A little over-ready, in fact . . .'

'Coming!' I eased my legs out and smoothed the cat's rough fur where it had ruffled in the night. 'Sorry, Pep.'

He purred and closed his green eyes.

I washed my face in the basin by the window, and stuck a tongue out at the reflection in the polished metal above Gabo's bed, straightening his sheets, dustier every day, but still made. The voice line arched next to his pillow – a long, thin hollow Da had etched for us up the walls and over the ceiling. When we pressed our lips to it and whispered, it carried our voices so we could talk even when we were at each end of the room in our separate beds.

Three years now. Three years since I sat there, my

twin's hand fire in mine as he faded in the night, fast as a blown-out match.

But still I could conjure him. Easy as breathing.

It would not do to start the day sad. Shaking the thoughts out of my head, I pulled on my school dress. It was as big as it had been six weeks before. My best friend Lupe would laugh. *Still the shortest in the class!* she'd say.

I quickly braided my unbrushed hair and hoped Da wouldn't notice I hadn't untangled it all summer. Pep was rolling on the bed but I wasn't allowed to stroke him with my uniform on. My teacher, Señora Feliz, was always picking ginger hairs off my dress with irritated fingers.

I pulled aside the curtain that served as my bedroom door, and carefully stepped over Miss La, who squawked as I scattered her small pile of crumbs. She narrowed her misty eyes and pecked at my ankles, chasing me further into the main room where we ate, talked and planned adventures.

A big bowl of blackened porridge sat on our large pine-plank table, marooned among a sea of maps. More of Da's maps were stuck to the walls, and they rustled as I passed, like a talking breeze.

I traced the papers with my finger as I did every morning, watching how the silver pigment of Afrik's rivers met those of Æygpt; how Æygpt clung to the curve of Europa Bay like one hand grasping another across the sea. On the opposite wall hung the sketchy coast of Amrica and its dragging ocean currents, labelled with strange, wondrous names: the Frozen Circle, the Vanishing Triangle, the Cerulean Sea. The paper was dyed a beautiful deep blue, and the currents were picked out in thread against it. Da had used a needle thin as a hair for these – gold for Cerulean, black for the Triangle, white for the Frozen Circle. But past the eastern coast, everything stopped. Only one word broke the blankness.

Incognito. Unknown.

I could almost feel Da's disappointment in the long-dried ink of the word. Unfavourable tides on his last trip meant an early return to Joya, and Da never again made it across that wild expanse before the Governor arrived on our island. Governor Adori closed the ports and made the forest that stretched coast-to-coast between our village of Gromera and the rest of the island into a border, banishing anyone who resisted his rule to the other side. Gromera was cut off from the rest of Joya, and the forest was strung with thick thorns and enormous bells to warn the Governor's guards if anyone came through. I had never heard the bells ring.

Da dreamt of filling in the gaps on his Amrica maps, whereas what I wanted, more than anything else, was to cross the forest border and chart the Forgotten Territories which lay beyond, though I had never told him so.

There was only one map that showed the whole of our island, and it hung in Da's study. I called it Ma's map because it had been passed down through her family for generations, maybe ever since Arinta's time, a thousand years ago. It had always felt like a sign that Ma and Da were meant for each other, that he was a cartographer and her only heirloom was a map.

Each of us carries the map of our lives on our skin, in the way we walk, even in the way we grow, Da would often say. *See here, how my blood runs not blue at my wrist, but black? Your mother always said it was ink. I am a cartographer through to my heart.*

'Fetch the jug, would you?' Da's voice made me jump, pulling me back into the room.

I dragged a chair to the shelves, carefully taking the jug from high up, and put it on the table next to the porridge. It was forest green and special, because it was the last thing Ma made. We used it only on the first day of school, and on birthdays and feast days. Da kept it out of reach and washed it with great care.

I could remember Ma, sometimes – dark-eyed and mostly smiling, smelling of the black clay she worked with, making pots for the villagers and delicate pieces for the Governor. Or maybe I imagined her, like the songbirds.

'Good morning, little one.' Da limped from the kitchen. I rushed to take the milk pail and cups he was carrying.

'You shouldn't walk without your stick,' I scolded.

Da had broken his leg as a young man, leaping from the jetty of an Æygptian port on to a moving ship, and now used a walking stick carved from a fragment of his great-grand-father's fishing boat. It was my favourite thing out of the many favourite things in the room. Light as paper, it floated in even the thinnest skim of water, but most miraculously of all it glowed in the dark. Da said it was because of the sap, but I knew it was magic.

I hurried to clear a space on the table, shifting the Himalay Mountains on to a shelf.

Da poured the milk into Ma's jug, then settled down on the bench next to me and grinned. 'Pick a pocket.'

I rolled my eyes. 'Left.'

He wiggled his eyebrows like two black caterpillars. 'Right answer.' He pulled a small jar from his pocket.

'Pine honey!' I unscrewed the lid and the smell filled my nostrils, making my mouth water. 'Thank you, Da.'

'Nothing but the best for your first day back at school.'

I shrugged. 'It's only school . . .'

'Oh, well, I suppose I'll just have to eat all of this myself, then . . .' He took the open jar and mimed pouring the honey into his mouth.

'No!' I grabbed it back. 'You're right, it's a very important day. I'm only surprised you didn't get two jars.'

The honey was so good I hardly noticed the porridge was burnt, but when I looked up Da's food was untouched. He was sitting in that hunched way that meant he was thinking. His hand rested on the milk jug and I could see the pulse in his wrist. His eyes had a faraway look.

First days of school were hard for both of us.

I cleared away my bowl as quietly as possible and pushed his closer to his hand. 'I'll see you later, Da.'

When he didn't answer I picked up my satchel and left the house, closing the peeling green door gently behind me.

CHAPTER
TWO

Our street ran in a straight, steep line down to the Western Sea, and all the houses were built the same: a long row of mud huts with straw roofs that Lupe thought looked sweet. I thought that they looked as if one good gust of wind would send them all tumbling into the water.

I normally ran to the market square, skidding downhill on my heels, because the ravens liked to fly low and running put them off. Today, though, I settled for a fast walk – after all, I was almost at the top of the school now. It didn't seem right to run like a little child.

Masha, who lived across the street, was standing in her doorway. I waved, trying to see past her into the house.

'Looking for someone?' She smiled, her lined face crinkling like old paper. 'Pablo's already left. You know the Governor likes them to be at work before dawn.'

Masha's son Pablo had been born when she was already

old, her belly swelling even as her hair turned grey and her face creased with age. Masha called it a miracle, and Pablo *was* miraculous. Gabo and I had always been in awe of him, as all the villagers were, because of his strength. Aged ten, he could lift his parents, one over each shoulder. Having a piggyback from Pablo felt like flying, but it had been a long time since I'd seen him.

Two years ago, when his mother's back got too bad, Pablo left school and took her place as a labourer, although Masha pleaded with him not to. Now fifteen, he pulled carts as if they were paper, and cared for the Governor's horses too.

'He took the present for Lupe,' Masha added, wrinkling her nose. I knew she didn't understand why I chose to be friends with the Governor's daughter. 'I told him to hide it like you asked.'

'Thank you,' I said. 'Maybe I'll see him tomorrow?'

'Maybe.' But her voice was not hopeful. He was always up before sunrise, home after dark.

I waved goodbye, shouldered my satchel and started down the hill.

From this high up Gromera looked like a wheel, or a starburst, with the market square at its centre and streets like spokes spiking outwards, some ending at the wide, calm harbour that bottlenecked into the sea, ripe with fish. On a clear night, the stars settled on its surface like water lilies.

The Governor's ship was moored there, as always. Da

said it was carved from a single Afrik baobab trunk. The baobab must be an enormous tree, because the hull nearly spanned the width of the port, the mast arrowing towards the sky, the sails stowed. It crouched over the fishing fleet like a mountain, huge and unmoving. Like everything the Governor had, it took up far more space than it ought to.

To the east, his house glinted in the sunrise. Built from black basalt and big as five ships, the mansion sat between the blue sea and the green forest, spreading out over the fields like a storm cloud. From here, though, it looked small enough to squash between my forefinger and thumb. Below it was the village, with the school halfway between.

The old school building had been small but bright, and we had painted the walls rainbow colours with whatever dyes Da could spare. But then the Governor had knocked it down – Lupe had decided she'd had enough of being taught alone at home and demanded to be sent to the local school like the rest of us.

Governor Adori had rebuilt it from stone, twice as big, because if his daughter was going, it had to look grander.

'Not for me, you understand,' Lupe had said with a sad smile. She adopted an even posher voice to add, 'To uphold the family honour.'

We weren't allowed to paint the walls of the new school. A lot of children were unkind to Lupe because of that, but I knew it wasn't her fault.

Behind the Governor's house, closest to the forest, was the orchard, where I had never been. I squinted at the ant-like specks of the labourers there, and wondered which one was Pablo. To the west, the black sand of the beaches was almost covered by the incoming tide. We were not allowed to be on the beaches at high tide, and no one was allowed in the water unless they were launching one of the Governor's boats. My toes itched. Da had described being in the sea but it was not the same as trying it for myself.

Above the beaches were the clay mines, which I tried not to look at because it brought back one of the few clear memories I had of Ma – the day she took Gabo and me to the mines. She taught us how to tie ourselves with vines to a dragon tree – *You knot like this, and then rub the sap into your hands for grip* – and lowered us one by one into the gorge. Gabo got scared and wriggled so much the knot broke. When he landed on the soft mud at the bottom it made a very rude noise, and he was filthy when Ma climbed up with him from the darkness. I laughed so hard it hurt.

I remembered that, that ache in my belly. How it came back two months later, when Ma died. Only then it was sharper, and there was no one carrying anyone out of that darkness. Three years on the same sweating sickness took Gabo. Three years after that, the clay mine memory still made my throat feel tight.

Lupe always met me by a barrel at the edge of the market square so we could walk to school together, even though it meant she had to get up almost as early as the labourers. When I got to the square a queue was already forming for the well. More and more people used it since the River Arintara began drying up.

All the stalls were open, selling fish and grain and leather. Most of the stalls belonged to the Governor, their cool blue awnings like a patch of sky, with the honey stall a bright sun-yellow in the middle.

As I made my way towards the barrel someone grasped my wrist. I jumped, stumbling against a nearby stall, and vegetables tumbled to the dusty ground.

'Hey!' the stall keeper growled. 'What do you think you are doing?'

I turned to see who was gripping me. It was a woman dressed in green robes, which meant she worked in the orchards. She should already be there – latecomers were sometimes whipped.

'I'm sorry,' the woman said to the stall keeper, without taking her eyes from my face. 'Isabella Riosse?'

'Yes,' I said. 'Who—'

'Something has happened.' She clutched my wrist harder. She was so small, her face almost level with mine.

'What do you think you are doing?' the stall keeper repeated, stepping out from behind his piles of potatoes.

'Cata,' hissed the woman, ignoring him. 'Have you seen her?'

I frowned. 'Cata Rodriguez?' Cata was in my class at school, but we had only spoken a couple of times before.

The woman nodded fiercely. 'I'm her mother. She said you were friends. I thought maybe you knew where she was.'

I shifted uncomfortably. It was true that I was nicer to Cata than anyone else, but she was very quiet and mostly people ignored her. 'I'm sorry,' I began, 'I haven't—'

'I've looked everywhere. She wasn't there when I woke up, I—' The woman broke off, breathing hard. Her hand fluttered to her chest, as if she could not fill her lungs.

'You! What are you doing here?'

Cata's mother jumped. One of the Governor's men was striding towards us, the crowd parting like wheat before his blue tunic.

'If you see her, send her home,' the woman said to me hurriedly, face twisted with worry. And then she was gone, running in the direction of the Governor's estate.

'What a mess,' tutted the stall keeper, starting to pick up the vegetables. 'No, don't help. You've caused enough trouble already.'

Dazed, I walked to the corner of the market square where Lupe and I always met. Something in the woman's face had shaken me, right to the bones. I hoped Cata was all right.

'Isa!'

I spun around as Lupe came running across the square, satchel flying. The other villagers shrank back from her. The Governor's daughter did not have many friends. Not that Lupe cared.

'I don't give a fig,' she'd said to one of the girls teasing her about the fussy plaits her mother insisted on. 'Isabella likes them, and that's enough for me.'

We made an odd set, Lupe and I: she as tall as a near-grown boy, and I barely reaching her shoulder. She seemed to have got even taller in the month since I had last seen her. Her mother would not be pleased. Señora Adori was a petite, elegant woman with sad eyes and a cold smile. Lupe said she never laughed and believed girls should not run, nor have any right to be as tall as Lupe was getting.

She squeezed me tightly and then drew back, eyeing me up and down.

'Still so short!' she said enviously, then frowned. 'What's wrong? You've gone all pale. Did your da not let you out in the sun this summer? Mama does that, but sometimes I sneak out—'

'Cata's missing.' I pushed the words out. 'I just saw her mother.'

'Cata?'

I rolled my eyes impatiently. 'The girl who sits at the back.'

Lupe shifted from one foot to the other. She had that look on her face, like Pep sauntering away from a broken dish.

I stared at her. 'What?'

'What, what?' said Lupe, pulling her satchel higher on to her shoulder.

'You know something.' I stepped forward.

'No, I don't.' She stepped back.

I raised my eyebrow the way Da had taught me.

Lupe wilted. 'I'm sure it's nothing. It's just, she was working in the kitchen this summer, and I asked her to go to the orchard for me yesterday, to get some—'

'The orchard!' The sick feeling in my stomach was back. 'Lupe, you know we're not allowed.'

'Yes, of course I know, but I hadn't had dragon fruit in *ages*. I needed to have them on my birthday, didn't I?'

I had never had dragon fruit and was not even sure what they looked like, but I did know they were Lupe's favourite, grown in the Governor's orchard at the edge of the forest. Out of bounds to everyone except his guards and a few of his servants.

'Lupe, you know that if Cata got caught, she's probably in the Dédalo right now.'

Lupe waved her hand dismissively. 'Still on about that place? I've never seen it, and I live there.'

It was typical that Lupe should not notice something right under her nose. And the Dédalo – the labyrinth – *was* right under her nose, because Governor Adori had built his house directly over the natural tunnels that were now his prison. Masha's husband had served a decade there before he died.

Lupe flung her arm around my shoulders. 'Come on, grumpy guts. Cata will be fine!' She began to propel me along the narrow street towards the fields. 'She'll already be in class, probably stuffing her face with my dragon fruit. I'll let you have some, they're so delicious. And don't forget the fireworks tonight!'

Lupe hated the dark, but she loved fireworks. They *were* extraordinary, with their beautiful colours and falling-star-shine, but they scared Pep too much for me to like them.

'Papa's let me pick the colours. There're gold ones, a blue one, two red ones . . .'

I let Lupe's voice wash over me as we took our shortcut across the fields. She was probably right. Even if Cata had been caught, surely the Governor's men wouldn't have thrown a girl into the Dédalo just for stealing fruit? I promised myself I'd be extra nice to Cata at school, maybe even invite her to watch Lupe's birthday fireworks from my garden. 'Oh, and you haven't seen this,' said Lupe, stopping suddenly and jerking me to a halt.

'What?'

Lupe untucked a thick gold chain from her dress and held it out on her palm. A gold locket glinted in the sunlight, engraved with a shape I recognized.

'That's Afrik, where Papa is from,' said Lupe. 'He gave it to me for my birthday. It was my grandmother's.'

'What's inside?'

Lupe shrugged. 'Da says I'm not allowed to open it until I'm older. He's the only one with the key.'

'It's lovely.'

'It's heavy,' said Lupe. 'But I like it. It was all I got, though.'

She looked at me expectantly. I tried to pretend I didn't know what she was waiting for, but she was grinning so stupidly I couldn't keep it up. I took out a scroll from my satchel.

'Happy birthday,' I said, grinning too.

'A map! Marked with an *X*!'

It was a very simple map, with no star lines and a compass that was only an arrow with an *N* on the end. I hadn't had time to make it a proper hunt with lots of clues.

'Treasure.' I squeezed Lupe's fingers.

'No point just standing there,' Lupe shouted, bounding ahead. 'Race you!'

With her long legs Lupe should have been the favourite, but she was as uncoordinated as a one-legged rabbit and so we ran together. My lungs filled as I ran across the dry field, bag slapping my side.

Cata will be at school, Lupe will get her dragon fruit, and everything will be all right.

At last Lupe reached the *X*, the abandoned rabbit warren where Pablo had hidden the present for me. Inside sat a small twist of blue paper. She unwrapped the simple plaited bracelet, made with leftover thread I had begged from Masha. Woven in amongst the multi-coloured strands was a single thread of gold I had stolen from Da's study. He never made special maps any more, so I didn't think he would notice.

'I love it!' Lupe wound it around her wrist and I tied the knot. 'It's my favourite present.'

Only Lupe would prefer a scrappy piece of string to a pure gold locket. It was another thing I liked about her.

'Come on,' I said, taking her sweaty palm and pulling her towards the low rectangle of school. Being late for the first day might be all right for Lupe Adori, but Señora Feliz would not forgive plain old Isabella Riosse so easily.

We broke into another run, hoping not to hear the bell, and arrived in a dead heat, panting and laughing, stitches needling our sides.

'I . . . won!' Lupe gasped.

'No . . . me! I . . . beat . . . you.'

'Girls!' Señora Feliz appeared at the school door, her face sour as a lemon. When she recognized Lupe, her face went as sour as two lemons. 'Señorita Adori! You should have been told, I sent someone straight to your father—'

'What?' Lupe frowned. 'Why?'

'There's been a— Well, your father will tell you, I'm sure. School is closed today.'

'Closed?' I said, stupidly. 'But why?'

'Enough questions!' snapped the teacher, then her face drained as her eyes fixed on something behind us.

We turned to see a carriage drawn by a pair of dun stallions picking its way slowly across the pitted path from the village. The horses seemed restless, sidestepping and shaking back their manes. Two men sat beside the driver, the sun glinting off their swords.

The carriage's blue curtains were drawn, protecting its passengers from the heat. But even at this distance, I could make out the broad Governor and his tiny wife, silhouetted through the silk.

CHAPTER
THREE

The carriage stopped outside the school. The driver jumped down to open the door as Governor Adori swept aside the curtains and stepped down into the dust. I shrank back, standing in Lupe's shadow. This close he was shorter than I expected, but wide-shouldered, his chest round as a barrel.

I had never met him before, seen him only on his horse in the annual parade, where the whole village was made to come out and cheer. The Governor's men even handed out blue banners to wave, and fined people if they got the cloth dirty. I wondered if he knew Lupe was friends with the cartographer's daughter.

'Come now,' he said to Lupe.

She looked uncertainly at me. I released her hand.

'Papa, what's—'

'No questions. Get inside.'

'Can Isabella come?'

I ducked my head as he peered past her. 'No,' he said. 'We're going home.'

'Can we drop her at the village then?' said Lupe uncertainly. I knew she was not allowed to invite people over.

The Governor clicked his tongue, then snapped his fingers in my direction. 'Hurry up.'

Señora Feliz tripped alongside us. 'Sorry, Governor Adori. I did send someone ahead, but the girls had cut across the fields—'

The teacher fell silent as the Governor held his hand up impatiently. He motioned for us to get into the carriage.

My legs shook as I climbed up into the soft interior and sat opposite Señora Adori. She shifted her skirts away from my dusty sandals. Her lips were pursed and she was even paler than usual, her blue silk fan flicking impatiently around her face. Da said she came from Europa, and she certainly dressed as if she did. Despite the heat she was wearing a full-skirted blue silk dress, and a bead of sweat was snaking its way down her cheek. She did not move to wipe it away.

We set off. It was my first time in a carriage but it was hard to feel excited. Why was school closed? And why had the Governor come to pick Lupe up? He never had before.

I chanced a look at him. He was imposing in the cramped space of the carriage, his skin darker than Lupe's, dark as Da's. His eyes were narrow, pupils black and slatted as a snake's, and just as cold. As I watched, a yellow dragonfly flickered briefly at his temple and he caught it mid-flight,

crushing it between two fingers and dropping it to the carpeted floor. I shuddered.

Why had he come here? Why did he treat Joya as if it belonged to him, and not to the people who had lived here for centuries? Because of him, I had never seen the rest of our island, let alone the world, and Da's skills as a map-maker were wasted. Because of him, there were no more songbirds. Masha said he was even to blame for the river drying up, but Da said she was just being superstitious.

It was stuffy and hot. The velvet of the seats stuck to my legs and I longed to throw back the curtain and see what was happening outside, but I kept my eyes fixed on a ring of keys glinting from his belt. Lupe seemed uncomfortable too.

'What's going on, Papa?'

The Governor's hand clenched and unclenched. 'Mama will explain when we get home.' His eyes flicked again to me.

'Is it something bad?'

He gave a hollow laugh, like a low, tuneless bell. Fear spiked through me. Why could he not explain now?

No one spoke again until the Governor barked out, 'Stop!' and the horses were pulled to a halt. The carriage rocked as the driver jumped down and opened the door. I drew back the curtain, and my skin chilled.

We were back in the market square, but it was deserted. All the stalls were closed and empty, apart from the feathery mass of ravens fighting over scraps. I didn't understand. This was usually the busiest time of day, when the villagers did their shopping before the worst of the heat swept Gromera's streets.

Governor Adori's voice was low and grim.

'Go home, girl. We can't take you further.'

'I'll see you at school tomorrow?' Lupe said as I went to open the door, a question in her voice.

'No school,' barked the Governor. 'Not for a few days at least.'

A drumbeat started in my chest. I wanted to ask what was happening, but my throat felt packed with sand. The Governor's wife again moved her skirts away from my feet. I took care to scuff my sandal on her silk shoe as I climbed down.

The Governor moved to pull the door closed but Lupe sprawled out and hugged me hard.

'I will try to find out what's happening,' she whispered into my neck. 'Meet me by the barrel tomorrow? At dusk? And don't forget the fireworks!'

I nodded as the horses were whipped into a trot, and she was dropped back into shade behind the curtain.

When I reached our house, I could barely breathe. The door was wide open, and the flowerpot by the door was tipped over, spilling earth and daisies. That stopped me short. The panic that had driven me up the hill was now holding me back.

'Da?'

Nothing.

I stepped forward.

'Da!'

The sunlight sent patterns whirling across my eyes in the gloom. I blinked them to a stop.

Da was not in the main room. It was the same as when I had left, the bowl of burnt porridge uneaten on its bed of maps. The walls swayed lightly – because of the maps or my spinning head I did not know. Only the forest-green jug had been moved back on to its shelf.

A rustle came from Da's study and relief filled me like air. That was typical of Da, too busy with work to hear me. He probably wouldn't even know what was going on outside. I crossed to the thick curtain and pulled it aside.

'Da—'

The shutters were open, letting through a breeze that lightly lifted the papers covering his desk. This must have been what I heard, because his stool was empty. Staining the parchment on the desk was something shiny.

Unable to stop myself, I reached out to touch it.

It was wet. My fingers were red.

I felt the room spooling away, my mind filling with dark.

Each of us carries the map of our lives on our skin . . .

Da's voice. Why was he speaking like that – cold, slow?

See here, how my blood runs not blue at my wrist, but black?

And why did I know exactly what he was going to say next?

Your mother always said it was ink. I am a cartographer through to my heart.

Da was ahead of me, walking through a dark channel of houses that swayed in the wind like trees. Now they *were* trees, and Da was stretching his hand towards me, redness flooding his palm. His chest was a bloody mess of skin and feathers, black feathers, like the ravens Pep caught.

My heart . . .

I was dreaming. Dream-Da was walking towards me, his face blank. I wrenched my chest from the hot ground, pulling myself backwards, away from him, along the stretching line of trees, out of the dream.

Something was tugging my hair.

Miss La. When I opened my eyes she squawked indignantly and began running around in circles. I was on the floor of the study. Pep was sitting in the doorway, regarding me cautiously. But Da – where was he?

My head throbbed as I looked at my fingers. Still that deep-red stain. I stood slowly. The room tilted and my shoulder ached where I had landed on it. I made my way shakily through the house, checking the kitchen and the garden, where Gabo's tabaiba bush was just beginning to bloom with starburst blossoms. Miss La and Pep followed, but there was no Da anywhere.

At the front the street was still deserted. I held on to the doorknob as if the ground were an ocean and letting go meant drowning. The drumming in my ears was back, layering over the sound of insects and the ravens that hunted them.

'Over here.' The voice made me jump. 'Isa, in here.'

Masha was peering through a crack in her shutters. I let go of the door and crossed the street, legs shaking.

Masha closed the door hurriedly behind me. 'What are you doing out there all alone?'

The words rushed from my mouth. 'It's Da, he's not at home and I can't find him and there's blood—' I held out my hand. It shook, though I told it not to.

'Isa, breathe.'

Masha wiped away my tears with her cuff, and steered me to a chair. She uncurled my fingers, and brought a bowl of warm water from the stove. She began rubbing at the stain with a coarse cloth. The back door was open and a sluggish breeze wafted in from the dirt courtyard.

'This isn't blood.' Masha's face was scrunched up with concentration.

'What?'

'It's not blood. See? See how it won't budge, no matter how I scrub it?'

The stain was still bright red.

'But what is it?'

Masha shrugged. 'Ink, I imagine.'

'But where's Da?'

A voice came from the back doorstep. I squinted and made out the shape of a broad back against the brightness. Pablo.

'I saw him heading towards the market square a while ago,' he said. 'He didn't look injured to me, just scared.' His voice was no longer boyish, but deep and cracking slightly at the edges.

Masha clucked her tongue. 'Why didn't you say sooner?'

I swallowed. 'Where was he going?'

'I expect to get you from school after hearing what happened.'

'What *has* happened?'

'You mean you don't know?' said Masha, her voice thin.

I shook my head desperately.

Masha and Pablo talked at the same time.

'Maybe we should wait until your da gets here—'

'They found a body—'

'Pablo!' said Masha sharply.

'What? She wants to know. She'll find out anyway.'

'You just want to scare her.'

'I won't be scared.' I jutted out my chin, to show I wasn't crying any more. 'You can tell me.'

Masha threw down the cloth she had been using on my fingers.

Pablo hesitated, then stood, stepping forward into the shade. 'This morning, a girl was found in the orchard,' he said at last.

Taking my silence for incomprehension, Masha took my

hand softly. 'He means, a girl was found dead. Killed.'

The silence unfurled until I forced myself to speak. 'Who?'

Masha paused, looking at Pablo. He was so much taller. Two years had stretched him high as a man. I wondered if Gabo would have grown the same as me, or faster.

'A girl called Cata. Cata Rodriguez.'

I looked at him for a long moment, feeling nothing, hearing him through the pulse in my ears. I pressed my palm to my forehead to stop the rising flood of questions. Masha took it, and held it between her own.

'Isabella, you need to rest.'

I opened my mouth to speak but Masha raised a warning finger. 'Not one more word. I know you are worried about your father but he is a clever man and he will be fine.'

I nodded dumbly.

'The Governor has ordered a curfew until they find . . . until they sort all this out.'

'Curfew?'

'We are to stay inside. Your da is probably stuck somewhere waiting for it to be lifted. He would never forgive me if I let you out of my sight. Not after a murder.'

A shudder ran through the three of us.

'I'll go home and wait.' I rose but Masha pressed me firmly back down.

'You will *rest*.'

The old woman stood and pushed past her son to reach the garden. I could see her picking something from a low shrub by the door.

Pablo turned towards me. His face was broad but no longer round, cut in angles around the cheeks and jaw. His eyes were the same dark brown, though. I looked down at my lap, suddenly shy.

Masha came back in and filled a cup from the water bucket.

'Drink this, and eat these.' She held out two small, dark berries. 'They'll help you sleep.'

'I don't need to—'

'You have had a terrible fright. Have some food and then you can lie down in Pablo's room until your father returns.'

'He won't know where I am!'

'I will keep a lookout at the window for him. I will not take my eyes from the street.'

Masha placed the berries on the table, watching as I picked them up and chewed. They sent out little bursts of bitterness that made my tongue tingle.

After forcing down the bread, I followed Masha to Pablo's room and got into bed. The pillow was soft and the sheets smelt of lavender, and as my body filled with heaviness from the berries, my thoughts chased themselves like dogs chasing their tails.

Cata, dead.

The orchard. Dragon fruit. Lupe.

Cata, dead.

CHAPTER FOUR

*B*ang!

I sat up, heart beating hard. Pablo's room was full of flames, but I could feel no heat.

Bang!

I looked out of the low window. The air sang with sparks, flung like a handful of rubies against the night.

Bang!

It was Lupe's birthday fireworks. I could smell them – smoky and sharp, tingling my nostrils.

Sulphur, Lupe had told me. *It's what makes them explode!*

I lay back down. The fireworks were over in another three bangs, painting the room blue and gold. As the last one fizzed away I heard whispers, low and urgent, filtering beneath the closed door.

My heart leapt as I heard the *tap-tap* of Da's walking stick, and then the rumble of his low voice.

'You're sure she's asleep? With all that racket?'

I squeezed my eyes shut. Whatever Da was about to tell Masha, he did not want me to hear, which meant that it was probably something I desperately *did* want to hear. I heard the door creak open a fraction, then close again.

'Fast asleep. I gave her something to help.'

'Thank you, Masha. Does she know about Cata?' asked Da.

I clenched the sheet at the mention of her name.

'Yes . . . I wanted to wait for you but Pablo told her.'

Da let out a long breath and there was a low mumble that may have been Pablo apologizing.

'She's all right,' said Masha soothingly. 'Where have you been?'

'I tried to send word but . . .'

Masha waited. I waited, too.

Da cleared his throat. 'Señora Feliz told me Isa had been taken home safely, so I joined a search party.'

'What about the curfew?'

'The Governor's not looking — we had to do something.'

'He didn't even cancel his daughter's birthday fireworks!' raged Pablo. 'What kind of person does that?'

Masha made a shushing sound. 'Where did you go?' she asked Da.

'To the orchard. We weren't allowed into the forest—'

'Why not?' interrupted Pablo. 'If I had just killed someone, I know where I'd go—'

'Hush!' Masha scolded, but Pablo pressed on, his voice

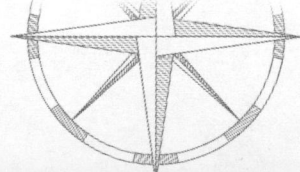

all edges.

'Adori doesn't care about Cata, does he?'

'Pablo!' Masha's voice was fearful. It was dangerous to accuse the Governor of doing wrong. People who did so found their livestock vanished then appeared in the Governor's fields, or found their drinking wells sullied with mud.

'The boy's right,' said Da. 'Adori's not doing anything. And I agree that whoever did this is likely to have crossed through to the Forgotten Territories.'

'Are there any clues?' Masha asked.

I crept out of bed and closer to the door as Da lowered his voice. 'They found marks around the body. Looked like claw marks to me, but there're no dogs big enough. Deep gouges, thick as my thumb. Maybe the murderer scraped the ground to cover his tracks.'

I couldn't listen any longer. I threw the door open.

Da and Masha were sitting together at the kitchen table, with Pablo standing by the window. Da stumbled to his feet, his bad leg collapsing slightly. He was dusty all over, with shadows under bloodshot eyes and red ink stains on his shirt. But he was here. He was safe.

I ran to him. 'Who did it, Da? Why isn't the Governor looking for who—' I forced myself to say the words, 'For who killed Cata?'

The three of them were looking at me with the same expression, as if they understood something I didn't.

My cheeks grew hot. 'Someone needs to do something!'

'Enough, child!'

I flinched and swallowed my questions. Da never shouted.

'Let's go,' he said curtly.

We crept the few metres home in a deep silence that was nothing to do with the curfew.

I carried Pep into my room and listened to Da tidying up. When he came in I pretended to be asleep, but he can always tell.

'I'm sorry for shouting, Isa. I shouldn't have. I just—' He sighed heavily. 'I'm tired. And sad, for Cata. Does that make sense?'

I made a small noise in my throat.

'I thought maybe I could say sorry with a story?' he said.

Pep mewled grumpily as I rolled over to face Da. 'Why won't you tell me what happened?'

'How about Arinta?'

It was my favourite tale – the myth of the saviour of Joya – and even though Lupe teased me for being too old for bedtime stories I loved hearing it. But I wasn't done being annoyed. I rolled back over and Pep hissed.

'All right.' Da sighed. 'I'll let you get to sleep.'

Before he could stand up I put my hand out behind me. 'I suppose a story wouldn't hurt.'

He sat back down, and when he spoke I could hear the smile in his voice.

'Arinta was a very brave girl. She lived at the centre of Joya a thousand years ago, when it was free from the earth and sailed the ocean like a living ship. There was no forested border, no Forgotten Territories, and songbirds sang in every tree.

'But one day, a fire demon that bubbled beneath the seabed noticed the beautiful floating island and wanted it for himself. His name was Yote. He was the length of a river and as hot as the sun. He built a column of rock to climb through, and caught Joya, attaching it to the seabed. The people of Joya were afraid. They knew he was going to claim the island for the Fire Realm and they would have to leave their home.

'Arinta was sad. She loved Joya, with its forests and sea and songbirds. So that night, she stole her father's sword and crept out of the house to where Yote was rumbling the earth, readying himself to swallow Joya. She journeyed underground through a waterfall, drenching herself in the water to protect herself against the flames, and walked until she arrived at Yote's lair. She called out. Yote heard her, but did not stop rumbling.

'Arinta did not give up. She attacked the rock walls with her sword to set the sea on him. Yote became afraid. He could defeat rivers, but the sea would swallow him up. He agreed not to take the island if she stopped. They swore to these terms and she left the sword embedded in the rock so he knew she was keeping her promise.'

Da hesitated. 'I think we should stop there.'

'But you always say you have to finish stories, even if they don't have happy endings,' I said, even though I had heard it so many times I could say the words along with him.

He spoke fast, the words blurring into each other.

'But while Yote was a lazy demon, he was also a proud one. He did not want the islanders to know a girl had outwitted him, but he could not destroy the island, for oaths bound demons for a thousand years. Instead he sent his fire dogs after Arinta and they chased her through the tunnels until she got lost.

'Arinta's father searched and searched the tunnels, but she was never seen again. Some say she became the river itself, others that she is still down there, her spirit making sure Yote keeps his promise. Either way, Arinta looks after Joya, her sacrifice a gift more powerful than any fire demon.'

CHAPTER
FIVE

'**M**orning, little one.' Da's voice was soft. 'I'm sorry to wake you. How are you feeling?'

I couldn't speak it aloud, the twist of worry that was knotted through my body. 'Fine.'

I sat up as Pep jumped off the bed.

'I'm going door to door today with a few of the others,' Da said. 'Asking if anyone saw anything.'

'What about the curfew?'

'Something has to be done. Don't worry,' he said hurriedly, smoothing out my frown. 'We didn't get caught yesterday, did we? And if you have any problems just call for Masha out of the window. Keep the door locked.'

I felt a stab of fear at the thought of being left, but Da was right. Cata deserved justice, and as long as Pep and Miss La were here I wouldn't be alone.

Before he set out, I bathed his leg and wrapped it tightly. The old scar ran jaggedly from his knee to his ankle, like a red vein. When he'd jumped aboard the ship in Æygpt, he didn't even know where it was heading. *For all we knew, we would sail over the edge of the horizon and never be seen again*, he explained, pointing to the oldest maps. Horrible beasts populated the eastern coast: gigantic fish with claws and scales striped like tigers, one-eyed elephants with fangs and tusks sharp as glass, creatures that to the cartographers of old were less terrifying than the unknown.

I had always found this strange – preferring monsters to not knowing – but now I understood. The murderer was out there, nameless and faceless. That was more unsettling than if the killer had been revealed to have four heads and teeth as long as knives. As Da left, I hugged him a bit tighter than normal.

'You'll be safe, Isa,' he said. 'Bolt the door.'

Da's study was full of treasures from his travels, but it was not the telescope from Europa nor the astronomy charts from Chine that fascinated me. It was what hung on the wall above his desk.

Ma's map of Joya. Made before the Banishment, before the Governor arrived, even before Da's family settled here from Afrik. Made when the island still floated. Da said that if Arinta were real – and of course I knew she was real – she'd have lived on a Joya that looked much like the one on Ma's map. Pep leapt on to my lap and settled down as I gazed up at it.

The fabric, a pale brown worn thin with age and use, was fraying at the edges. The map was basic at best, and focused on odd details. Gromera was shown as the tiny settlement it must once have been. The Marisma, the swamp, was stitched in blue thread with the forest circling it. A blue star marked Arintan, the waterfall through which Arinta was said to have descended to meet Yote.

There were six villages, dotted irregularly around the coast; Carment was the one furthest north. The very centre of the map was blank but when held up to the light it seemed faintly lined, like the veins of a leaf.

I wondered what the rest of Joya looked like now. Overgrown, maybe? And what about the people the Governor had banished when he arrived, and those from the other villages? The rest of Joya might be completely empty, for all we knew.

I scratched Pep behind the ears, then pulled a sheet of paper towards me from the pile of used pieces Da kept for me. Da had been teaching me cartography since Gabo died. It was an obvious attempt to distract me, but I had grown to love it. I dipped a quill into the blue inkwell – I didn't even glance at the red – and began to draw what the Forgotten Territories looked like in my head.

My legs had gone numb before Pep finally stirred, jumping off my lap and stretching. I flexed my fist, examining the half-finished map. The scaling of the forest was wrong, but I was happy with the detail of the river bends.

Pep mewled. It was past his feeding time. Dusk was falling outside. I frowned. There was something to do with dusk I had to remember . . .

My stomach jolted. *Lupe!*

I didn't think twice about breaking my promise to Da.

The market square felt just as eerie as it had the day before, like a village taken by spirits. Ravens chattered and fought on the roofs.

Across the deserted stalls I saw Lupe, sitting on the barrel, long legs trailing from beneath a pink taffeta gown. She looked as if she was on her way to a ball.

Lupe waved. She didn't seem scared.

I scuffed my way to the barrel.

'I was worried you'd forgotten!' said Lupe. 'Good idea to arrange this, right? Did you see the fireworks?'

I nodded. She sprang off the barrel and spun around. 'It's so quiet. Isn't it strange?'

'Everything's strange.'

'It's about to get stranger,' said Lupe, stopping suddenly mid-spin. 'Guess what?'

'What?'

'We're going on a trip!' said Lupe, flinging her arms out.

'What do you mean?'

'I *mean*,' said Lupe, obviously deflated by my tone, 'Papa and Mama and I, we're going on a trip. To Afrik.'

Afrik? I tried to make the words sink in. The Governor was leaving? 'When?'

'Soon!' said Lupe happily. 'But you can't tell anyone. Papa said it was a secret.'

'Only a trip? You're coming back?'

She nodded, more curls slipping loose from her bun. 'Papa would have said if not, wouldn't he?'

Would he? 'How are you going?'

Lupe grinned, pleased to have shocked me. 'On that.'

She pointed to the Governor's creaking ship in the harbour below, but I couldn't drag my eyes from my friend's face. She felt like a stranger.

I knew Lupe lived differently to others, knew this made her selfish sometimes. But she was also kind, and normally the silly things she said didn't make me want to walk away and wish I had never known her.

'What's wrong with you?' asked Lupe. 'I thought you'd be excited for me—'

'What's wrong with *you*?' I hissed. 'How can you act like this, with Cata gone?'

'Gone where?'

'You don't know?' I said, my temper running through me like needles. 'Why there's no one around, why there's a curfew?'

'Papa doesn't tell me things like—'

'Did *Papa* forget to mention the detail? Too horrible for his darling daughter to hear?'

'Why are you being so mean?' Lupe asked, her lip

wobbling.

'Cata's dead!' I shouted, sending ravens spiralling. 'Because you sent her to the orchard, and someone killed her!'

The words, spoken out loud, were as shocking to me as they were to Lupe. Her face went almost as pale as her mother's.

'I didn't know—'

'No, Lupe, you choose not to know! You don't care about anything, anyone, outside your life. You don't understand about your father, about Cata, about *anything*—'

'I do care. I want to know! Tell me – no one tells me anything!'

We had never argued before and Lupe's eyes were bright, but I didn't care. I felt threaded through with rage, as though if I could keep talking, keep hurting Lupe, I would hurt less myself.

'Because of you sending her to get you dragon fruit, Cata was in the orchard the same night as someone bad. Because of you, she's dead and she's not coming back. And because of your father, we won't find who did it. He's too busy sorting out your fireworks to do anything. He won't send a search party through the forest, which is where everyone says the murderer went—'

'Th—the forest?' stuttered Lupe. 'Why won't he? Why won't he go?'

'Because he's a coward, and rotten right through. Because everyone in your family is rotten and ever since he came here everything is rotten.'

Lupe was crying now, holding her stomach as if I had punched her. My nails stung crescents into my palms. I felt powerful, anger pushing out the fear.

'My Ma died because of you coming here, and Gabo. Your *papa* stopped us crossing the forest to get medicine. And now Cata's dead too, and you're just running away. You're all running away to Afrik and leaving us with your mess. Well, good.'

'Isa, I—' Lupe was holding her arms out to me but I kicked dust at her skirt.

'Go! Nobody wants you here.'

Lupe looked at me, face scrunched up, tears thick on her cheeks. And then she was tripping over her gangly legs, sprinting away towards her house.

I kicked the barrel, hard. My toe bent back and I gasped, collapsing in the dirt. The anger left as quickly as it had come, leaving a hollowness. What had I done? I hugged my knees, wishing I could take it back, all of it. Lupe hadn't known, hadn't realized . . .

'Isabella?' It was Pablo, his hand outstretched. 'Are you all right?'

I squeezed my eyes shut until I was sure I was not going to cry, then took his hand. He pulled me up so strongly I lifted off the ground.

'Sorry,' he said, then looked down the alley where Lupe had run. 'Wasn't that the Governor's daughter?'

'Lupe.' I sniffed. 'We're friends from school.'

'Friends?' Pablo arched his eyebrows. 'Didn't seem like it.'

I rubbed my aching toe. 'I said some things . . .'

'I heard. Did she say they were going somewhere?'

'To Afrik, on the Governor's boat. I—' I stopped abruptly, remembering Lupe had asked me not to tell. But I had said worse things. 'I should apologize.'

'Don't,' said Pablo. 'Let her calm down. You should get home.'

I let him propel me across the square, and as we turned up our street I noticed a livid bruise on his forearm.

'What happened?'

He looked down and shrugged. 'One of the horses kicked me. They're in a strange mood these past couple of days. The goats too – when I left they were all bunched up against the gate.'

'Why?'

He shrugged again. 'Don't tell my ma, she'll be on about omens and the like.'

It was the longest conversation we'd had in years, but as we fell into step on the slope, I realized how easy it was to be silent with him too, like the years and Gabo's death had momentarily spun in on themselves and we were walking back, the three of us, after a day by the sea. I wanted to say this but Pablo's face was set.

About halfway up he said, 'We should go quicker, it's almost dark.'

The sun was falling. Ravens crouched on every roof.

Their numbers seemed to have increased since the murder, as if they were multiplying, filling the absence of people on Gromera's streets. I kept my head down. The dust glowed orange and then faded to a deep navy by the time we reached my green door.

Pablo knocked and it opened a crack. Da's worried face peeked through, and then he threw the door wide. 'Where were you?'

'Sorry, Da. I—'

'No note? Do you realize how worried I've been?'

'He's leaving,' Pablo broke in. 'The Governor. He's going to take that ship and leave us in this mess.'

'Might be better if he went,' Da said.

Pablo shook his head. 'He can't get off so easily. We have to teach him a lesson—'

'Not now, Pablo.' Da glanced pointedly at me.

'You're coming with me?' Pablo persisted.

'No.'

'I'll be all right on my own—' I began.

'Enough, Isabella.'

I glared back, and Pablo disappeared without another word, leaving a stony silence in his wake.

CHAPTER
SIX

I looked up at the ceiling. Something was different, and I was not sure whether it was good different, or bad. Sunrise had bled into the room, turning the mud walls yellow. The air felt close and lay over my body like a hot, sticky sheet. The silence was too complete, and there was a strange smell, like Da's burnt porridge but more bitter.

Pep was sitting in the far corner of my room. He flinched when I got up to stroke him. His fur was up, his tail bushy like he'd been in a fight.

'Pep?' I murmured soothingly, but he hissed and slinked under Gabo's bed. Still in my nightclothes, I left the room. Da was sitting at the table, rubbing his eyes. He looked exhausted.

'Da?' My voice was hoarse with sleep. 'There's something wrong with Pep. He seems frightened. Or grumpy with me.'

'Miss La too,' said Da, jerking his head towards the

kitchen. I could hear her flapping her wings against the sides of her coop.

'She's always grumpy.'

'No.' Da looked haunted. 'Something is scaring them.'

I looked into the kitchen. There were feathers bunched by the back door, and scratch marks at the bottom, like Pep or Miss La or both of them had been trying to claw their way out of the house. My stomach turned.

'What happened, Da?'

Someone coughed from the garden, making me jump.

'It's only Masha,' said Da soothingly. 'She came over to tell me.'

'Tell you what?'

He shook his head slowly. 'Something bad happened last night, Isa.'

The back door opened and Masha came in and sat down heavily. She did not look at me.

'I don't understand it,' continued Da. 'But I think Pablo might've been mixed up . . . He's all right,' he added hurriedly. 'But him and Goraz and some of the others. They . . .'

'They did a very stupid thing,' Masha finished for him.

I dropped down on to the bench opposite them. 'What?'

'They should have just let the Governor go,' said Masha, dazedly. 'Why does revenge always win over common sense?'

'Hush, Masha,' said Da.

My heart began to thud. It was my fault. I had told Pablo

that Lupe had said they were going.

'What did they do?'

'I went to see myself,' said Masha, her voice almost a monotone. 'It's a bad sign, you mark my words. Something else must follow. The last time I saw anything like that was when the songbirds—'

'Please, Masha,' said Da. 'Enough.'

'That's what it is, though. An omen. Because Pablo said the animals were nothing to do with them. Just the ship.'

'The animals? The ship?' Before my brain could catch up with my body, I slipped on my sandals and unlatched the door with trembling fingers.

'Isabella, no!' Da was struggling to stand up, his bad leg buckling beneath him as he grasped for his stick.

I didn't wait for him.

Ahead, smoke was laddering from the harbour. I began to run.

People were crowding the water's edge and that same sharp smell filled the air, mingling with the smoke, catching my throat.

Slowly, the smouldering water resolved itself into something else. The charred remains of the Governor's ship, the hull blackened, the sails ash.

Pablo's words floated back to me on the acrid smoke. *The Governor. He's going to take that ship and leave us in this mess ... We have to teach him a lesson ...*

Ravens were circling like a cloud of flies. Breath ragged, I reached the first of the villagers and began to push through to the front, ducking under arms and around legs. Though I had dreamt for years of the day I would stand in the sea, I didn't stop to enjoy it. As the first waves began to soak my nightdress I looked down.

A tide of dead animals stretched before me, filling the harbour: cattle, horses, chickens and goats ... all stamped with the Governor's brand. His animals, drowned. The ravens had already started swooping.

Had Pablo and his friends done this, too? I could not believe they had. As my knees buckled, strong, rough hands cupped under my armpits and began dragging me back through the throng.

Then came other sounds: loud voices, shouts, screams. People were struggling with the Governor's men, their blue uniforms bright against the grey and brown clothes of the villagers. I tried to shrug off the hands that were still pulling me away, but their grip was firm.

It was Pablo again, his face somehow aged. He picked me up and ran. Others were running too.

I craned my neck around Pablo's shoulder, and saw the whole, horrible scene laid out as if time had stopped: the bay, full of drowned animals, blood on the sand as the Governor's men got out their whips and dragged people into caged prison carts.

I shut my eyes, wished I could unsee it all, but the

red-black shift of the waves burnt behind my eyelids.

Then Da was speaking close in my ear, a door was being opened and his hand was stroking my head as I was carried past the whisper of the maps and placed on my unmade bed.

'Damn leg, I couldn't keep up with her.'

'I should go. They'll be coming for me.'

'Was it you? The ship, the—'

'The ship, yes. But the animals . . . all we did was let them loose. We didn't chase them into the bay.'

'I believe you. I had to cage Miss La and put Pep in the study. They kept trying to get out.'

'I need to leave.' I heard Pablo striding to the door, but before he opened it there was a heavy knock. I sat up.

'Who's there?' I could hear the nerves in Da's voice.

There was no answer, only another loud knock.

'Run!' Da hissed. I heard Pablo stumble against the bench as he bolted for the back door just as the front door was kicked open.

A man in Governor's blue strode inside. Tall, with a scarred face and thick eyebrows pulled low over icy blue eyes. He was drawing back his arm, his whip rippling behind him, but I shouted and Pablo turned, ducking just as the whip came down with a *crack!* on the table.

Pablo launched himself at the guard, barrelling him to the floor and ripping the whip from the man's grasp, throwing it across the room. Pablo had just raised his arm when Da held his fist.

'Go!'

Pablo hesitated for a moment, then ran for the front door, which was hanging off its hinges, only to stop dead and back slowly into the house. Masha appeared, a lump swelling on her wrinkled forehead. Another man in blue was holding her arms behind her back.

Pablo seemed to shrink. The first guard was on his feet now, spitting blood on to the floor. Pablo offered his wrists to the manacles the guard unlooped from his belt, and took the slap that followed with only a grimace.

Masha was released and instantly began pleading. 'Please, he's only a boy!'

'Silence!'

Masha bit her hand, shaking her head. The guard was holding out another pair of manacles.

'She hasn't done anything—' started Pablo.

'We have our orders.'

A third guard was wrenching Da's hands behind his back.

'He wasn't there either.' I ran forward. 'He was home, with me—'

'I can't leave my daughter alone,' said Da, struggling, but no one was listening.

'Please,' I sobbed. 'Don't take him, he didn't do anything. Please don't—'

The man drew back his arm and Da shouted, 'Isabella, no!'

I backed away as they were pushed roughly out of the

door. The two men holding Pablo were eyeing him warily, but I knew he would not try to escape. Not with his mother threatened.

My body felt numb, my tongue latched. I could not let them take Da, but I could not see how to stop them. They were bundled into the prison cart, Da wincing as he climbed the steps. I ran back into the house, scanning the room for his stick. It was propped against the wall and I grabbed it, shoving it through the bars and into Da's hands.

But the first guard, the one with eyes like ice and the whip, had seen. He wrenched it from Da's hands and broke it squarely across his knee. The stick splintered and dropped in pieces to the ground. The cart set off fast down the hill as I knelt in the dust, gathering the fragments together.

I did not know what to do with myself. Our house filled with the smell of the Governor's burning ship as I sat on my bed with the broken stick and cried. I cried so hard all my body was sore and my eyes puffed. I felt completely empty. I sat there until I heard Pep mewing mournfully from Da's study.

The cat was back to normal, rubbing himself against my calves. Miss La seemed to have calmed down too. She pecked my hands when I opened the coop and I fed them both, then went into the garden so I did not have to listen to the silence of the house. Not even the maps were whispering.

Smoke still hung in the air and I imagined the ship, the sails and mast fallen like clipped wings. That was what the Governor was so angry about, why all those people had been arrested at the harbour. Why they'd taken Pablo and Masha and Da. A dead girl was less important to him than his boat.

Pep came outside too and I watched him chase flies until my stomach started to rumble. I picked an orange and went inside. Halfway to Da's study, I saw something fluttering by the front door, slid between a crack in the broken wood.

A note, short and obviously written in haste – the ink was smudged and the paper had been folded before it had dried, leaving a ghostly reflection above the sentences. The sight of Lupe's careful handwriting made something swell in my throat.

Isa,

I hope you find this. I'm going to show you not all Adoris are cowards. I'll show you I'm not rotten.

I'm going across the forest to find who killed Cata. Maybe when I get back we can be friends again.

Love, Lupe

xxxxxx

P.S. Check under the pot. It's for you to look after.

I looked left and right, but there was no sign of her.

No, that wasn't quite true. I peered at the dust. There were hoof prints leading up towards the forest. So not all the Governor's animals had ended up in the bay. She had a horse.

A faint ringing started in my ears, swelling around the other noises – the far-off murmur of the sea, the rustle of ravens on the rooftop above, my own jagged breathing. How far had she got? I had been in the garden for hours, the whole afternoon gulping by.

My hands began to shake as I opened the door and lifted the pot, pulling out a thick chain. Lupe's locket.

Now a roaring filled my ears.

I'll show you I'm not rotten.

I had done this. And now I had to fix it.

CHAPTER
SEVEN

I closed our broken door as best I could, sliding to the floor. The threads of problems dangled in front of me, and I tried to think of a way to weave them into a solution.

I had to go after her. And for that I would need a horse too – where from, I had no idea. And anyway, if anyone saw a girl out alone near the forest after what happened to Cata, they'd surely stop me. Maybe they'd already stopped Lupe . . . I took a deep breath. She couldn't have gone far. Not Lupe, with her taffeta gowns and easy laugh, crossing to the Forgotten Territories?

Pep sauntered over, rubbing his head against my limp hand.

'What do I do, Pep? How do I fix this?'

He pawed my hand until I stroked his back, ginger fur wafting in the air. I paused and he nudged me with his head, but I watched the hairs floating until an idea started to form. It was not one I wanted, but no others came.

I stood and crossed to the kitchen, where Miss La was asleep in her coop. Taking a knife to my bedroom, I wrapped my plait twice around my hand and pulled it taut. Then I began to saw upwards, slicing roughly. Some strands were pulled out, breaking before the knife reached them. The pain was like sparks popping against my scalp.

Finally, the plait came away and fell on the floor. My head felt light, dizzying. I hacked at the longer pieces until I was left with something resembling a boy's haircut.

Gabo's chest crouched in the opposite corner and I heaved it open, a cloud of dust mushrooming as the lid banged the wall.

Coughing, I dressed quickly in a faded cotton tunic and trousers, pulling a jacket over the top. They were short at the wrists and ankles. So much time had passed, inches of time since they had last been worn. I took a deep breath and looked into the polished metal.

Gabo blinked back at me, his eyes wide with astonishment. The next moment he had gone, and I turned away, heart pounding, mouth dry. The broken pieces of Da's walking stick were on Gabo's bed, glowing with their strange light.

Picking out the largest piece, I wrapped it in my discarded dress. Something like that could come in handy. Lupe's note went in my pocket, her locket around my neck. *I'm coming, Lupe.*

Da had bolted the shutters in his study. I lit two candles,

which made circles in the dark. Even though it was a rescue mission, I could not waste this chance to map the Forgotten Territories.

Emptying his satchel of books, I began to fill it with his cartography equipment: ink, quills, paper, a leather pad to mark miles, a compass, dragon-tree sap for repairing shoes and ripped maps, two drinking flasks. Then his weapon, bought in Afrik: a flat, curved blade, serrated at the edges like teeth.

Finally, carefully, I took Ma's map of Joya from the wall. I rolled the map into a tight scroll, wrapped it in a piece of soft cloth and nestled it next to the fragment of walking stick. I carried the now-heavy satchel back into the main room. Pep was sitting on the bench.

'Listen, Pep,' I said. He rolled on to his back, waiting for his tummy to be rubbed. Cats never understand the gravity of a situation. 'I have to leave you alone for a while. But I'll leave the back door open and plenty of water bowls, and you'll be all right, won't you?'

My eyes were pricking with tears but I knew he would be fine. He was a stray until two years ago, and was always catching mice and ravens. Seeing the tummy rub was not forthcoming, he yawned and jumped off the table, slinking through the gap in the broken front door.

'Goodbye, then,' I said feebly.

I filled my drinking flasks and then all the bowls in the kitchen with water and food, and propped open the back door. Miss La woke up as the breeze ruffled her feathers and began pecking at the latch. I was about to open it when there was a firm knock that pushed the front door further off its hinges. The next knock sent it crashing to the floor.

Two men stood in the doorway.

'Sorry about that,' said one, not sounding very sorry. 'It was almost like that when we found it.'

I nodded. I hadn't practised my boy voice yet.

'Your mother in, son?' the other man said kindly.

I shook my head.

'Well, we won't be too much bother. Just got to collect any chickens you have.'

'Why?'

'The Governor's going on an expedition and—' the first began.

'Official Governor's business,' interrupted the other. 'Needs supplies.'

'An expedition?'

'His girl's gone missing. Lupe.'

Her name twisted my stomach. The Governor knew she was missing. He was going after her.

'No chickens,' I croaked.

Miss La, on cue, emitted a piercing squawk.

The kinder man gave me an apologetic smile as the other pushed roughly past. 'Governor Adori's orders. Wait a minute . . .' He frowned at the map-covered walls and table. 'This the cartographer's house? The one in the Dédalo?'

I nodded. 'He's my father.'

'Ah.' The man shifted as I heard the catch on Miss La's

coop slide open. 'Have you been told?'

'Told what?'

'Your father, he's—'

'Let's go,' said the other man as he emerged from the kitchen. Miss La looked at me indignantly.

'He's what?' I said, heart thumping.

'We'll be gentle with her,' said the kinder man, ignoring my question and taking her softly in his hands.

'Cook won't be,' sneered the other.

'Hush!'

But I had stopped listening. I felt numb to it all. What had the guard been going to tell me about Da?

They left me alone in the whispering room, thinking.

The expedition would not leave without the chickens.

If I beat the chickens back to the Governor's house, the expedition would not leave without me.

The late afternoon sun danced on the crystals of the Governor's basalt mansion, smudging it into a shimmering mirage.

One night, not long after Ma died, Da had taken me and Gabo to the cliffs to sit and watch the moon throw light off the house.

There are two kinds of crystals, he'd told us. *One is granite, a light-coloured rock. And, like you two, it has a twin, a dark version of itself. Its name is 'gabbro'. After* that, I had called Gabo 'Gabbro' for a while. He hadn't liked it.

As I got closer, the satchel slapping my thigh, I saw that even the windows glinted – the Governor had had huge sheets of glass made from molten Gromera sand. A room at the front corner of the house was filled with people. Voices drifted across to me through an open window. Two guards stood by the dark wood door. I had not thought this part through. What if no one would let me in?

I crept to the open window.

'We are wasting time here, we need to get after her!'

'It's not a waste, we have to plan this—'

'—and how do we guarantee your daughter's safety?'

'—madness, who knows where she is—'

I took Lupe's note from my pocket and ripped off the top and bottom so it read:

I'm going across the forest to find who killed Cata. Maybe when I get back we can be friends again.

Love, Lupe

xxxxxx

I peeped inside. There were about a dozen men in Governor's blue, crowded around a large ornately carved table. No one was looking my way.

Without stopping to think better of it, I pushed my satchel through the window, and tumbled in after it.

CHAPTER
EIGHT

I must have knocked whatever was holding the window open, because it slammed shut as I hit the floor. Hard. The men turned and stared. The silence was sudden and terrifying, stretched wide as a cave.

'Who are you?' said someone eventually.

My voice would not come. Scrambling to my knees, I stared at the floor. It was covered in carpets depicting animals and hunting scenes. I moved my knee from the neck of a swan in mid-flight.

'I—'

'Did you just come through the window?' said another.

One of the men standing at the back of the room near the fire threw his arms up in a gesture of exasperation. 'Speak up! Who are you?'

'I'm sure he just came through the window.'

I tried again.

'I – I have this.' I brought the crumpled note from my

pocket. 'It's from Lupe.'

All the men seemed to hold their breath.

'Is this a joke, boy?' rumbled a low, considered voice.

For one wild moment, I thought it might be Da, but when the crowd parted it was the Governor himself. My throat constricted, and my heart beat so loudly in my ears I was sure he would hear it.

He was sitting at the head of the ornate table, papers spread before him, face as thunder-dark as his house. He stood up and I hurriedly dropped my head. Only days before I had sat opposite him in his carriage. I was counting on the fact that he had barely deigned to look at me in those tense minutes.

'I said, is this a trick, boy?'

'N-no.'

'Why would my daughter be writing to you?' The voice was low and close now. The newly cropped hairs at the back of my neck lifted. Again I focused on the bunch of keys at his belt, glinting silver and gold. 'And not to me? Look at me when I'm speaking to you.'

I did. For a painful second, I thought I saw a glimmer of recognition in his black eyes, but it was gone in an instant. I held out the note.

The Governor scrutinized it, then looked up, eyes narrowed. 'Why would my daughter be writing to you?' he repeated.

'She sent it to my sister. Isabella.' I didn't think the Governor would like Lupe being friends with a boy. 'They're

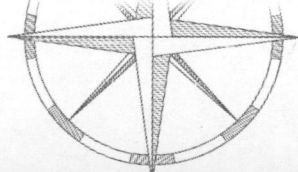

friends. From school,' I said, deciding to stick as close to the truth as possible.

'And did she give this to you herself?'

'No,' I said. 'Yes. I mean – she left it for us to find. I came straight here when I did.'

'Are you sure this is not fake?' said someone pompously. 'Why would your daughter tell this boy's sister, and no one else?'

'Who are you?' said Governor Adori, slowly, ignoring the man.

'Gabo Riosse. I'm the cartographer's son.'

Governor Adori raised his eyebrows. 'A man with ideas above his station.'

'His thoughts are very low at the moment,' quipped another man. 'Down in the Dédalo.'

The laughter spread again. I kept my eyes on Governor Adori. He was looking at the note, considering.

'It is not a fake,' he said decisively. 'Which means my daughter at least left willingly. That is something to be thankful for. But we have wasted enough time talking. How many horses did you collect, Vasquez?'

'Nine,' said Vasquez.

'Nine?' the Governor roared. 'Nine is not nearly enough! My daughter is missing, I need a large search party—'

'Sir,' said Vasquez carefully. 'That is all we have. The others . . . the harbour. They all belonged to you.'

Adori began pacing back and forth like a caged animal, flexing his fists and muttering to himself. Finally he said,

'Well. Nine men it is.'

'We will need to take the horse boy, they're all still spooked.' I flinched. It was the man who had taken Da. 'Don't know what's got into the beasts.'

Pablo. My chest loosened slightly at the thought of seeing him.

Governor Adori smacked his hand against the wall. 'Enough problems! What do you not understand, Marquez? My daughter is gone!'

My chest ached for Cata, gone for ever.

'And this boy's father,' said Vasquez coolly. He seemed used to the Governor's rages. 'Can't leave without a navigator. We'll need to find water, maybe shelter. Know where to avoid . . .'

I took a deep breath, thought quickly. Da could not go to the Forgotten Territories. He would never be able to ride with his bad leg.

'I thought you might say that, sir. I brought his cartography tools.' I held up the satchel.

'That cripple? On a horse?' sneered Marquez. I was happy to see that Pablo had left him with an ugly yellow bruise on his cheek.

'What option do we have?' snapped Adori. 'Would you have us wandering the Forgotten Territories lost?'

'Me,' I said, loudly.

'What?' said Adori.

'I can navigate, sir,' I said, emboldened by the silence that fell across the room. 'I'd be more use to you, sir. Than my da, I mean, with his leg being bad. And I have a map, an old one of the Forgotten Territories, from before . . .' I swallowed, 'before they were forgotten,' I finished lamely.

The Governor raised a finger and the room fell silent. His beetle-black eyes were still locked on mine.

'Can you read maps, boy? Can you draw them?'

'Yes, sir. My father has trained me.'

'Prove it.' He clicked his fingers and there was movement behind him. A small desk and chair were brought forward. The chair was shoved into the backs of my knees, and a piece of paper and ink placed before me. 'You came through the fields, yes?'

'Yes.'

'Being a cartographer, you will know the current positions of the stars.'

It was one of the first things Da taught me. *Stars are the earliest maps, the most precise. They can tell you where you are better than a compass – after all, they have a bird's-eye view. If you can learn to read the stars, you'll never be lost.*

'Then map the route from here to the square. I want buildings – accurately scaled – field boundaries, the location of north, a wind indication, an estimation of time, walking and on horseback. Do it. Quickly.'

He strode back to the table and the men closed ranks around me, watching. Some of what he was asking was a task for a navigator, not a cartographer. But I knew Da would be able to do it easily, even in the darkness of the

Dédalo. I picked up the reed quill and, closing my eyes, retraced the journey behind my eyelids. The night sky danced on them, the stars fixing their positions. I opened my eyes and began to draw.

The Governor was talking again. 'Vasquez, you are to take up the governorship while I am away.'

'I'm greatly honoured,' Vasquez simpered.

'Sir, wouldn't it be better if you stayed?' said Marquez. 'I hardly think Vasquez capable of controlling Gromera in such an uncertain state—'

'An uncertain state?' said the Governor icily. 'We have locked up the usual troublemakers. Any more, and Vasquez simply has to lock them up too. Do you doubt my judgement, Marquez?'

'Of course not,' he blustered.

'You expect me to stay behind?' Adori's voice was rising.

'I was merely expressing—'

'Then don't. Stop expressing. Just do as I say. Understood?'

I assumed Marquez nodded, because no one else spoke, or raised further objections. The route was blossoming like a tabaiba bush beneath my hands; small black buds of buildings, and branches of boundaries. I added the ant-lines of wind as I remembered it, snaking off the sea, south-easterly and warm.

I was just starting the criss-cross of star lines when the Governor's attention returned to me. 'Are you done yet, boy?'

I hastily scrawled an estimate of time in the corner before the paper was snatched from me. The Governor regarded it coolly, then said, 'Marquez, fetch Ferdinand.'

The man left the room as the Governor looked down at me.

'Can you ride a horse?'

'Yes.'

'Can you follow orders? Do you know when to speak and when to be silent?'

I nodded vigorously, to show I did.

Governor Adori rocked backwards slightly on his heels, his eyebrows knitting.

'How old are you?'

It was not a question I had been expecting. I was about to say thirteen, but something stopped me. Lupe was thirteen, too. Adori might think of her if I said my real age, and might not let me go. Pablo was fifteen, but so tall and broad he would pass for a man. Best to settle for somewhere in-between.

'Fourteen, sir.'

'Small for fourteen,' sniped Marquez, but Governor Adori nodded.

'I didn't much like the idea of taking Riosse with us anyway. He's old and disrespectful, and that leg is a hindrance.' He turned his back. 'You'll do.'

Hardly believing it, I said, 'Sir, I thought that if I came with you, maybe my father could—'

'Don't push your luck, boy.' The Governor's voice sent

shivers spidering across my back. 'If you do not disappoint me, we'll see about your father.'

The door opened and I saw the kind man who had fetched Miss La.

'Go with Ferdinand to fetch the horse boy. You two can saddle up the horses.' He turned to the man. 'Watch them. If they try anything, put them both in the Dédalo. And send Luis here, I want him with us. Oh, and Ferdinand?'

'Yes, sir?'

'Don't let him see Riosse. I don't want him starting any trouble down there.'

'Yes, sir. Come on, boy.'

I allowed myself to be led out of the room into the dark hallway, the tide of voices rising again. I had done it. I was going.

Ferdinand led me along a corridor. 'Why didn't you say you were coming here, eh? Could have given you a lift.'

I could tell he was trying to put me at ease, but my skin was crawling with nerves. The Governor's house seemed to go on for ever. The floors were covered with tapestries, muffling our steps.

The Governor's blue was everywhere. Even the ceilings were like a sky. It seemed such a waste. Da always had to ration his sea-colours, and yet here there was enough blue dye to make a large-scale map of Afrik's rivers. Most of the walls were covered with paintings of stern-eyed men and ships. There were so many candles, wax burning down and no one using the light.

At last we reached a place where the corridor intersected with another, like a crossroads. At the centre was a trapdoor fitted with a heavy metal lock. I swallowed hard. The entrance to the Dédalo.

A guard stood over it. He frowned as we approached.

'What's going on?'

'You're needed in the drawing room, Luis,' said Ferdinand curtly.

The guard left without another word. It was strange, I thought, how they followed orders without comment or question.

Ferdinand took a key from his belt and stooped to unlock the trapdoor, turning the key slowly and with great effort. The bolts slid noisily.

The man heaved, veins in his neck straining as the trapdoor creaked open. He let it fall to the floor with a bang, wincing at the noise. A terrible smell rose from the entrance below: damp, rotting. In the thin light of Ferdinand's lamp, I could see a stone-cut staircase leading into an impenetrable blackness. It made me dizzy just looking at it.

He climbed gingerly down the first few steps, then seemed to remember he was not alone. He stopped, and climbed back up, taking chains from his belt.

'Nearly forgot,' he said, holding out the chain.

He locked my wrists together, and fixed the chain to a bolt in the wall, next to a heavy-legged table. I shuddered. How many people had been locked here before descending to the Dédalo?

I watched as the lamp became a pinprick of light, fading as Ferdinand went lower, towards Da, somewhere below me.

I looked around, eyes catching something above the table.

A large butterfly was resting on the sky-blue wall, its wings outstretched. They were an iridescent purple, edged with black. I had never seen a butterfly that size or colour before. I leant forward, taking care not to move too fast.

It was not until I was breathing close enough to rustle the wings that I saw it was behind glass, saw the pin through its heart.

CHAPTER
NINE

I leant heavily against the table leg with my back to the butterfly until Pablo's exhausted face came into view. His hands were tied behind him, his clothes filthy. He was dragging his feet, squinting as he stepped into the light of the corridor. His eyes widened when he saw me, but thankfully he said nothing as Ferdinand unchained me.

We followed the guard in silence, crossing a small courtyard to the stables. Nine horses were lined up inside. I could tell they were not the sort of horses the Governor was used to. In fact, I was quite sure that one of them was a donkey.

'No trouble, you two. I'll be just in here.' Ferdinand indicated another door. The smell of cooking wafted out. 'Don't worry, that's not your chicken!' he said to me. 'She's in one of those boxes there. Had to put her in a separate one – she kept pecking the others.' He pointed to a stack of wooden crates. I grimaced. Miss La would not like being squashed in like that, alone or not.

'We need all of that, on those,' Ferdinand continued, nodding at the horses.

Pablo raised an eyebrow. 'You're taking live chickens?'

Ferdinand shrugged. 'The men like to eat fresh. And I wouldn't keep them waiting.'

He untied Pablo's hands and went inside.

I waited until the door closed, then turned quickly to Pablo. 'Is Da all right?'

'Why have you cut your hair?'

'To come here.'

He sniffed. 'Looks all right.'

'I don't care how it looks. How's Da?'

His face was inscrutable. 'Why are you here?'

'How is he?'

'Well enough. Goraz is looking out for him.'

'And Masha?'

'Not too bad.'

'You're sure?'

'Your da is all right, Isabella. You should worry more about yourself.'

He began to lead the horses out into the courtyard. I went over to the crates and started trying to locate Miss La.

'What happened? The night the animals—'

He turned, eyes flashing. 'That was nothing to do with us!'

'I know that, but do you know how . . .' I couldn't find the words for what had happened in the bay, and anyway I didn't want to make him angry. He hadn't had a temper when I'd known him before.

'No,' said Pablo. 'But the others talked about it a lot, in the Dédalo. They think it's something bad.'

I snorted. 'Well, obviously it's something bad.'

'No, more than that. Not just bad.' He swallowed, a muscle in his jaw working. 'A bad omen. It means something else has arrived, to make the animals run to the sea.'

He sounded just like his mother.

'Didn't you see anything when you were out with Goraz?'

It was Pablo's turn to snort. He started saddling up the horses, each movement smooth and well practised. 'That was part of the problem. We couldn't see anything. The Governor's men sneaked up on us in the dark, surrounded us. I nearly ran off the cliff trying to escape.' He leant his head against the mane of a bay mare, so his voice became muffled. 'It was awful.'

'What else happened? How did you get to the ship? Wasn't it guarded?'

He looked up sharply. 'It wasn't my idea. The fire drew the watch to the bay, and when we were running towards the house I almost believed we could do it.'

'Do what?'

'Get the Governor.'

'"Get" him?'

'Look, are you going to help?'

He began lifting the crates and strapping them to the horses. I tried to lift one. He took it from my arms with one hand, like a toy.

'What would you have done? If you had "got" him.'

'The Governor? I don't know.' Pablo shifted uneasily. 'Everyone was so angry, so fired up . . . I think they would have killed him.'

'But that wouldn't have helped anything. Cata would still be dead.'

'No more than she is already.'

'Lupe's gone after her,' I said.

Pablo nodded. 'The guard explained. I don't understand why you're coming with us.'

'It's my fault.'

'The argument you had?'

'Yes.' I frowned. 'Do you think we're going to kill the person who killed Cata if we find them?'

'Yes.' I flinched at his certainty. 'This isn't going to be fun, Isabella. Some of the men who saw Cata's body reckon it was more than one person.'

I wasn't sure I wanted to hear this but I didn't want to seem scared. 'What do you mean?'

'They think it was a group who killed her. Sounds to me like it was an animal. It was . . .' He hesitated.

'What?'

'Messy.'

I willed myself not to blink.

'All right.' He shrugged. 'Your da would never forgive you if he knew what you were doing, though.'

'I know.'

'I should tell them.' He nodded towards the door.

I put on my fiercest face. 'You won't.'

'I could.'

'You'd go in your ma's place, wouldn't you?'

'It's not the same thing—'

'It is the same, same as you taking her place in the fields.'

He paused a moment. 'Yes. But I'm a man.'

'You're a boy. And so what? Girls can go on adventures too.'

'Have you ever heard of a *girl* going on an adventure?'

I flushed in the darkness. I had only heard of one. 'Arinta.'

'She wasn't a very good heroine, though, was she? They ate her,' Pablo said.

'What?'

'The fire dogs, they eat her at the end.'

'No, she stays down there to protect us.'

'That's working out well,' said Pablo. 'And anyway, it's a story. In a story you can decide what happens at the end.'

We stared at each other in annoyed silence until he blinked and continued lifting and strapping crates. Suddenly he gasped and sucked one of his fingers. It was bleeding.

'Ouch! This chicken pecked me!'

'Miss La!' I peered through the slats of the box. A misty eye stared back. I laughed in relief. 'Can we strap this one to my horse?'

'Which horse will that be?'

'The smallest one, I suppose.'

Pablo rolled his eyes. 'You and that chicken.'

I opened the top of the box a little and put in some of the horse's feed.

An irritating grin played at the corners of Pablo's mouth. Then he asked, 'What do you think we're going to find? Across the forest?'

The Forgotten Territories. How many times had I lain awake thinking about what they might be like?

'More forest. The River Arintara . . .'

'I know the Forgotten Territories are real – I just never thought I'd actually see them,' said Pablo. 'Or that they'd have trees, a river. They always seemed made-up somehow.'

I knew what he meant. Not much could have changed in the three decades since the Banishment, but the way everyone talked about the Forgotten Territories, they might as well be a different country.

'What am I meant to call you?' Pablo said.

'What?'

'What am I meant to call you in front of the others? Isabella isn't a very manly name.'

'Gabo.'

Pablo's voice softened. 'Gabo.'

The kitchen door banged open. 'You two done?' called Ferdinand. 'The Governor's ready. Lead the horses round to the front.'

The Governor and another five men were waiting there, with Señora Adori in her usual blue. As the Governor kissed her goodbye I noticed her face was blotchy. I dropped my head, hoping she was no more observant than her husband.

The Governor chose a white mare and assigned the others their horses. I was right about getting the smallest horse but I was still too short to mount it, so Pablo lifted me, roughly slinging me on to the gentle bay. His hands were coarse, dry skin grating my arms.

The horse responded to the lightest touch, which was lucky, as I had only ridden a few times. Miss La stopped squawking as we settled into a trot, and when I peeked into the box she was asleep.

We turned our backs to the sea and cut across the empty fields straight towards the forest, which even in the slow brightness of dusk was clearly visible above us. My breath came in small, tight gasps. I tried to take deeper breaths as the waving, shifting smudge of the forest grew higher and more solid as we approached.

The muggy night fell quickly. My back was already aching from the lilt of the horse, and my feet itched in Gabo's boots. I longed for my light, well-worn sandals, left by our broken door.

Pablo was riding at the back. He had not spoken at all since saddling the horses, and I did not want to risk slowing to talk to him. Marquez kept turning around in his saddle to sneer at me to keep up.

We approached the banks of the Arintara, the river that spanned the island. I glanced back at Pablo through the shadows, but he scowled and looked away. I glowered too. Perhaps this was how boys looked at each other.

We forded the river, and I realized this was the furthest I had ever been from home. I thought of Da, still in the Dédalo, and felt a pang of guilt, but shook it off.

Hadn't I always wanted this? The map of Joya lay in Da's satchel, with its blank expanse at the centre. I was going to see what it held. Da had never bothered with his own island, too intrigued by what lay across the sea, but I knew he regretted it. Now I would draw it so he could see it too. A shiver of excitement ran up my spine until I noticed Marquez staring. I quickly adopted Pablo's scowl again.

Since the Banishment, the border forest had been re-inforced with high thorn bushes strung with the huge warning bells. As we got closer, I noticed some of the bushes had been trampled, and the ropes connecting the giant bells had been severed. They lay on the ground like metal hillocks.

'The bushes, they're trampled in this direction,' said Marquez. 'I think Jorge was right about the killers being the Banished.'

Governor Adori nodded. 'We go through here.'

But no one moved. I looked at the path. It looked like a herd of animals had passed through. Da had described claw marks around Cata's body. Perhaps this was another attempt to disguise footprints?

A chill ran through us like a gusting breeze, as if we had all realized for the first time why we were here, in the gathering darkness, about to cross into a part of Joya that had been forgotten for a generation. It was unknown, unmapped, and home to a murderer.

Da's flat blade with its sharp teeth, weighted the satchel. I wondered if I would have the courage to use it. I couldn't even throw stones at ravens. Then I thought again of Cata, and Lupe. If Lupe could go into the Forgotten Territories, I could too.

Gesturing for the men with torches to go ahead, Governor Adori glanced back at us all with those slatted black eyes, then turned and rode into the forest.

The FORGOTTEN TERRITORIES

Braque

Gris

Latitude 28° 08' 03" N

Longitude 17° 14' 27" W

10   20   30   40   50

CHAPTER
TEN

I t was hushed in the forest. The horse-high bushes stopped sound the way water does, and the torches' light threw everything into shadow. After a couple of the men had drawn swords on nothing more threatening than a branch, Governor Adori ordered them to put out the torches. My eyes quickly adjusted, and I felt safer knowing we could not be seen as easily.

The route was clear – the trampled bushes, leaking pale sap, were the only break in the undergrowth. I imagined Lupe, alone and determined. *I'll show you I'm not rotten.*

I was not needed to navigate while the path was so obvious, so I took out the compass, peering at it through the gloom. Despite fearing for Lupe, I could not ignore that I was in the Forgotten Territories at last. I would make a map Da would be proud of.

Every hundred strides the horses took, I marked a line on the soft leather pad I held in my palm, and every time the compass indicated a change in direction I scored under these lines with an arrow showing the new bearings, consulting the stars the way Da taught me. This was map-making at its most basic, but it was clear the others would not stop and wait for me to take more accurate measurements. I would just have to rely on memory when it came to drawing up the map. That was how I did it with Lupe on our treasure hunts through Gromera's narrow streets.

My hand was at my throat before I could stop it, feeling for the locket through my tunic. Marquez narrowed his eyes and I clasped the reins. Maybe it had not been the best idea to bring it with me.

None of us spoke for a while. The Governor's shoulders were set, and he hardly moved with the lilt of his horse. He obviously wanted to go faster, but the darkness and the narrow path made it impossible.

After a few miles the horses started to move more cautiously, shaking their heads and whinnying softly. The men drove them forward, digging the spurs on their stirrups into the animals' sides. My horse stopped completely until Pablo hit it sharply on the hindquarters.

It was a few more miles before any of us realized what was wrong. Finally Marquez spoke up.

'What's happened to the trees?'

We pulled our horses to a stop. The surrounding trees did not look alive. The leaves were like lace, criss-crossing blackly over tangles of dead branches. I squinted at one, holding my hand behind a leaf. My skin showed through, a lighter dark, webbed by the leaf's veins. Up close, the trunks looked like rock. As though the forest had been fossilized.

Forest fires were nothing new on Joya. Da said this small death was needed; that the trees grew back greener, stronger, gave more fruit. Even the scrubland that backed Gromera occasionally smoked and burnt.

But this?

This was different. The leaves hung on their stalks, skeletal and black, yet still attached. The broken bushes oozed black sap, as if the trees were feeding off darkness instead of water.

A light breeze ran over my exposed neck, a smell hooking into my nostrils. Something sharper than smoke . . . It reminded me of the scent that had filled Pablo's room after the fireworks.

What was it Lupe had said? Something from Asia . . .

'Sulphur?' Governor Adori spoke the word quietly, almost to himself, but in the dead air of the night it reached us all.

'Boy, come here.'

I glanced across at Pablo, but he shook his head. Governor Adori was looking straight at me. I nervously nudged the mare towards his horse.

'That map you have, the old one . . . Does it suggest this . . . change?'

Without a torch nearby, the inside of the satchel should have been impossible to see, but the wood-light, the piece of

Da's broken walking stick, was shining softly through the thin fabric of my rolled-up dress. As I made to pull out the worn map of the Forgotten Territories, thick fingers closed roughly around my wrist.

Marquez had dismounted, his face illuminated by the glow from the bag. 'That . . . What's that?' Without waiting for an answer, he reached into the satchel. He quickly touched the fragment, as if testing it for heat, then pulled it out, sending maps and instruments falling to the forest floor.

As he held up the glowing wood, its pale light was cast further and the men shrank back. The Governor dismounted, dropping heavily to the ground.

Swinging my leg clumsily over the mare, I half-fell to retrieve the papers and tools before they were trampled by hooves or the Governor's boots.

I crouched down, silently cursing myself for allowing the fragment to be found.

'Well? What is it?' repeated Marquez, as he passed it to Governor Adori. 'Why does it shine like this?'

'I don't know.'

'But where did it come from?'

'My father.'

'Before him?' asked Adori.

'I don't know,' I lied. 'It was passed down to him.'

Without commenting further the Governor slipped the wood-light into his belt beside his keys. I reached out, but Marquez pulled me back by the shoulder, fingers digging hard into my shoulder. My eyes watered and, blinking rapidly, I dropped my arm.

The Governor looked at me expectantly. I glared back.

'The map.' Pablo's voice was quiet, but still made me jump. He had dismounted and was holding out a pile of papers.

Mouthing thanks, I riffled through with shaking fingers and found the map scrolled in its sheath of cloth.

'Well?' The Governor was still staring. 'The trees?'

I examined the parchment, then shook my head. It held no clues, the key just showed the forest to be a mix of dragon and pine trees. I wondered how I would show the black trees on my map.

Marquez tutted impatiently. 'How much further does the forest stretch?'

I glanced down again, checking the scale against my leather pad. It was inaccurate, but not by much.

'At least twenty miles in that direction.' I pointed west. 'More if we go straight.'

'And how far to water?'

My fingers brushed the blue star that marked the waterfall. 'Twelve.'

The Governor nodded. 'Take us there.'

'The trees are starting to thin,' said Marquez. 'We won't have a path to follow much longer.'

'Lupe would look for water,' said the Governor, indicating the dried-up bed of the Arintara.

No, I thought. *She's not that sensible. She's looking for the killer.*

'Sir,' ventured Marquez, 'don't you think it would be better to stop for the night, and rise at first light? She's unlikely to be far ahead, and surely she would have stopped to rest.'

'If she has, it's all the more reason to continue, Marquez,' snapped the Governor. 'We could catch up.'

'The men are tired, sir,' said Marquez cautiously. 'If we encounter danger, we will need our strength.'

'And what of my daughter's safety?'

'She would be better served by rested men and rested horses,' continued Marquez. 'We can start tomorrow at a gallop, we'll find her by sundown.'

I wanted to carry on, but with every blink my eyelids felt heavier.

Finally, the Governor straightened his broad back and spoke to us all.

'We continue.' His glare cut short the murmurs of the men. 'And I suggest we pick up the pace.'

I carefully replaced the papers and instruments in the satchel, rolling the map back into its cloth. When I looked up the group had already moved on. Only Pablo was there, holding the reins of my horse.

'Ready?'

I nodded, grateful he'd stayed behind. Chancing a smile, I reached out for the reins. Instead he handed me a bundled piece of cloth. My dress.

'It fell out of your satchel. Put it away. Quickly.'

Pablo threw me across the saddle and pushed the horse forward before I had even sat up.

'Thank you—'

'Just pretend a bit better,' he snapped. 'The only reason no one sees is because they don't care enough to look.'

In first hours of daylight, the landscape was even stranger. Black forests had never been mentioned by Masha or the other elders, nor in Da's stories or on Ma's map. What had happened here, to make the trees' colours fade? It couldn't be the drought that made the plants grow like this. The wheat in Gromera was still gold, not grey.

We rode on for a couple more hours, uninterrupted and quiet except for the horses and the scratch as I marked every hundred paces on the leather pad.

Every line brought us closer to Arintan. Butterflies swooped in my stomach as we neared the waterfall. Pablo and Da might think it was just a story, but Arinta had always given me courage, and I needed that now.

We rounded a thick copse of trees, and my heart sank. No Lupe, and no cascading waterfall. Only the cracked bed of the River Arintara running low and sluggish.

'This is the mighty Arintan?' said the Governor, voice thick with disdain. The others dismounted but I nudged my horse forward.

Around another bend, a rocky overhang rose above my

head. A weak trickle ran over the edge, and behind it was a cupped space, a cave, which would have been hidden from view were the waterfall as full as in the stories.

My knees jarred as I dismounted. Tethering the reins to a tree, I waded into the river, Gabo's boots sloshing and stirring up mud, and walked into the cave.

The space was deeper than I first thought. The entrance was small and low, but at its darkest point was a wide passage, leading to another cave where I could stand. I stumbled blindly, feeling my way forward.

The walls were dry and oddly warm. I could feel strange horizontal lines on the back wall, as if the rocks had been laid flat together. It made me think of a game Gabo and I had played, singing and layering hands over one another faster and faster, drawing the bottom hand out and trying to be at the top when the song ended.

My breath caught. Missing Gabo always crept up like this. I would not allow it.

Feeling my way back into the open air, I scooped some water into my hands and drank. It was not the magical waterfall of Da's stories, but at least there was water.

I refilled my empty water flask and put it in my satchel, bringing out the full one from home and placing it on to my belt. Da always said it was important to use the staler water first on a journey, however tempting it was to drink the freshest.

The Governor and his men were settling on the river-banks. I sat next to Pablo on a boulder. 'What's happening?'

I whispered.

'We're going to have something to eat. Stopping an hour at the most, he says.'

'And then?'

Pablo shrugged. 'Then we keep going. I'd sleep if I were you.'

But I suddenly didn't feel tired, even though we had ridden through the night and past sunrise.

The Governor was standing a little apart, scanning the ground. Looking for traces of his daughter. He didn't seem able to stay still, as if his anger was turning into hot coals beneath his feet. Guilt churned sharply in my stomach. His eyes flicked towards me, and I looked quickly away.

'Runts,' called Marquez, snapping his fingers. 'Fetch some wood.'

I stood up, placing the satchel on the rock. I managed to find only a little kindling, but it didn't matter because Pablo emerged from the forest with an enormous bough of what looked like a dragon tree, black like the rest.

The men laughed, clapping him on the back, but his face remained set in a scowl. A fire was soon heating up a pot of stew made with chickens brought by the cook. I shuddered when I passed the pile of plucked feathers, and as the smell wafted through the air I fed Miss La, grateful she was here, a piece of home, grateful even for her pecks.

As the stew began to bubble, I decided to start on my map. But the satchel was no longer on the boulder. Had one of the men mistaken it for their own? My gaze trailed to the river.

The satchel was bobbing there. Heart pounding in my ears, I plunged my hands into the water. The satchel sloshed as I opened it, fingers trembling over the buckles. Papers and quills twisted and floated inside, and I upended it like emptying a disappointing catch from a net.

Ink had run from Da's star chart and stained through several sheets of blank paper. It was now a mess of black and red, barely legible. It would be impossible to create an accurate map if I couldn't cross-check the stars' positions. But that was not the worst of it. Ma's map was damp and stuck together. I held my breath and peeled it open. Surprisingly, it opened easily.

But this was not the map I remembered.

The drawings of forests were gone. Instead, the blankness at the centre was full of thick lines, the ones I had seen faintly when I had held it up to the light. They looped and crossed as the silk of a spider's web does, or the channels of a maze. In fact, the more I looked the more I was certain that this was what it was. But some of the lines ran through the area we had just crossed, and there had been no sign of roads there.

Perhaps it was the ancient layout of Joya? No villages were marked and, apart from the lines, the only shapes were circles dotted about the edges. At the centre was another circle, larger than the others, and drawn in red. This was the only colour on the map.

I hurried over to the fire and held the map up to see

more clearly. But the lines dissolved back into the paper, like ink in water, and disappeared.

'No!'

Marquez looked up at me, frowning. I traced them desperately, chasing them up the map even as they faded. The familiar shapes of the forests were reappearing, along with the names of the villages. Within a few seconds the map was back to normal.

I was certain I had not imagined it, though what had happened was so fantastical it belonged in one of Da's stories. What made the map change?

It was wet when the hidden layer emerged, and when I held it close to the fire it changed back. Now it was dry. I fumbled for my flask, pouring water over the surface.

Nothing happened.

I tipped the flask over the map again and again, but still nothing happened.

'You didn't imagine it,' I whispered to myself firmly. 'It was real.'

'Boy,' said Governor Adori suddenly, making me jump. He jerked his head. 'Come here.'

Pablo raised his eyebrows as if to say, *Hurry up*.

I walked shakily towards the Governor.

'I thought we'd find her here. I was sure she could not be far ahead.' His voice was low but dangerous, shaking slightly. 'Which way now? Which way would she go?'

It was obvious he wasn't talking to me. I waited, the map's transformation slipping from my mind. Lupe would go wherever the horse took her. I hoped she wasn't too afraid, as the adventure wore off and fear crept in. I felt breathless at the thought of her somewhere in the black forests, and a killer somewhere out there too.

'The villages,' said the Governor in a louder, decisive voice. 'Which is the closest?'

I looked carefully. 'Gris, sir.'

He nodded. 'Gris it is. You'll be ready to lead us there?'

'Yes, sir.'

'And you're working on a new map?'

I thought of the smudged star chart and sodden paper. 'About to start, sir.'

'Good. Don't make me regret bringing you.'

He turned his back, and I considered myself dismissed.

'What is it?' asked Pablo quietly.

'We're going to Gris. A village.' I wondered what we would find there.

Cook clanged the side of the pot with his spoon and shouted, 'Ready!'

Governor Adori was the first to eat. He ate by dunking bread directly into the pot, and after he had eaten his fill the others fell on the food like starving men. I could hardly eat a chicken stew with Miss La so close, and lost my appetite completely after one of the men started eating so fast the food came out of his nose.

I moved off to the riverbank to try to start work on the map. Da's voice rang in my ears as I laid out the pots of ink, damp quills and measuring devices.

The trick is leaving the space for what you don't know. Any man can draw where he's been – only a cartographer knows how to draw it to fit with where he's about to be.

I leant the satchel carefully on a nearby rock and selected the driest piece of blank paper. I stretched it on the ground, holding down its corners with rocks, then took the marked pad of leather from the pocket of Gabo's trousers and placed it next to everything else.

Before I started to draw, I looked around at the trees, casting shadows even in the early morning light. I tried not to imagine something looking back at me. Taking a deep breath, I dried the nib of the reed quill on my tunic, dipped it into black ink, and began to draw a new map of my island. It would not stay forgotten.

CHAPTER
ELEVEN

Consulting Ma's map, I took them north-west to Gris, hoping Lupe's instinct would be the same as the Governor's – to get out of the forest and back towards the coast.

'Don't get us lost, runt,' Marquez sneered. My fingers shook as I traced the path.

We followed a spine of rock that ran from the waterfall's overhang, creating a natural break in the trees and opening up a channel that the horses could travel along easily. It was a claustrophobic few hours, with the grey of the rock wall towering on the right and the grey of the tall trees rising to our left. Even the sky was unusually hazy. The whole world seemed sifted through ash.

Finally, the forest began to fade, and we broke out on to a wide pebble beach, the metallic glint of the sea unrolling beside us. It was soothing after the forest, and also meant we only had to keep watch on one side, with a clear stretch to the treeline.

It was easier to chart the distances with a view of the curving coast. The slow count to a hundred became effortless and my mind wandered, sometimes to Da, mostly to Cata and Lupe. The beach was silver in the sunlight, and the horses' hooves skittered as they grew used to the change in surface.

Out on the horizon, storms flashed over the sea, so distant we could not hear the rumble of thunder, only see the rolling clouds and the flashes of light forking up. I thought of the storm that carried off Great-Great-Grandfather Riosse's boat, and wondered if he had been so far out into that wild sea.

The ocean here seemed different, though really it was all connected and part of the same body of water. It was cartographers like Da who parcelled it up on paper and named it, to make it easier for explorers and traders to mark it as their territory. Just as the Governor had marked Joya.

Governor Adori brought us to a halt about a quarter of a mile away from where the map showed the village of Gris to be.

'All right, men, be on your guard. Marquez, you come up front with me.'

Marquez rode up the formation, hissing as he passed, 'Stay out of the way.'

'We advance slowly, then charge,' continued Governor Adori. 'So if we encounter anyone – anyone other than my

daughter – we put them on the defensive, make them flee. Stay on your horses until I give the order. If you are separated from the group, follow this ridge back and wait at the river. Understood?'

The men nodded. Pablo's face was grim, his hand tensed around his small knife. The Governor motioned for us to continue. I squeezed my heels. The mare blew out through her nostrils and moved forward.

The horses began to trot. Ahead, a wall broken by an arch marked the village boundary. Governor Adori kicked his spurs into his horse's sides. I heard the unmistakable crack of Marquez's whip on the flank of his stallion.

I flicked the reins and leant up out of the saddle like Pablo said to. The horses broke into a gallop, and as the men yelled I felt my blood rushing through me. We pounded through the arch, the yell dying in my throat when I saw what lay beyond.

The village was gone.

Only the crumbling fragments of mud walls and cracked streets remained. In a doorway was a sun-bleached skeleton, an adult's, arm and hand outstretched towards a smaller formation of bones. My own arms felt leaden as I tried to will the bones into something else. A shadow fell across my neck but there was no one behind except Pablo.

The Governor jerked his horse to a stop and dismounted in one fluid movement. The village had been razed, and at a glance it was obvious we were alone. The sea murmured beyond the houses, the blue of the men's tunics the only colour nearby. Bones and clay snapped under boots and hooves, but I was careful not to tread on anything.

Together we led the horses to what was once a village square much like Gromera's. As we reached the centre, a voice rang out.

'Stop!'

We spun towards Pablo, still mounted on his horse.

He pointed at the ground. 'Look.'

We followed his gaze. Under our feet ran a thick black line. I glanced around and saw another line intersecting it where the Governor stood, forming an X that divided the square. Scattered over the cross were white seeds.

I reeled back as I realized that it was dried blood that marked the X. The men shouted and ran from the cross, pulling their horses with them and scuffing the dust from their feet. But that was not the worst of it. Those pale objects were not seeds at all.

They were teeth.

The Governor stepped forward and picked one up, laying it on his gloved palm to examine it. A hush descended.

Pablo dismounted and stood beside me, so close I could smell a faint trace of the lavender Masha washed their clothes with. I looked skywards into the unrelenting grey, waiting for Governor Adori to speak.

Finally he said, 'These are not human. At least, not like any human teeth I've ever seen.'

He held out his hand and Marquez strode over. Both

men regarded the tooth, and Marquez took it and nodded.

'Heavy, too,' he agreed.

The tooth was passed around the others. Not wanting to take it in my bare hand, I looked at it lying in Jorge's palm. It was shaped like a dog's tooth, only sharper, the serrations deep and irregular. The root was blackened, as if the gum were diseased. I swallowed and looked away.

'What happened here?' Marquez spoke almost to himself.

I looked around. Judging by the rubble and the bones, the village and its inhabitants had been destroyed years ago. But was it possible the cross could lay undisturbed all that time? The ravens that flooded Gromera's streets would surely have scavenged here.

Something clicked into place. Scanning what was left of the roofs, and the far-off forest, I realized I hadn't seen a single raven since entering the Forgotten Territories. No animals at all – not the wolves that had once stalked the forests like a plague, and no sign of the deer or boar Da said used to be abundant on the island. Like the songbirds, the ravens had gone.

'Pablo—' I turned just as something far behind him moved. I focused on the spot, hoping it had been a trick of shadow. But it moved again, towards the horses now. Low to the ground, almost as dark as the cliffs behind it, moving with a slow, rolling gait.

Fear flashed through me, and my feet were released as if cut from a rope.

'Over there!'

The Governor's men reacted fast, standing back-to-back at the centre of the X, forming a circle with each man facing outwards, holding his weapon ready. There was a moment when nothing moved. Then they flooded from the forest.

We were suddenly surrounded, my vision blocked by broken walls and shadows.

'Protect the Governor!' Marquez yelled.

I thrust a hand inside the satchel and gripped the handle of Da's weapon. I let the bag drop to the ground as I pulled out the blade.

It was not a moment too soon. I caught only a glimpse of a dark grey body before being thrown backwards. I slashed the air.

All around was noise. The Governor was barking out orders, the chickens emitting high-pitched clucks from the cages lashed to the cook's saddle. The horses were baying and through the white edges of panic I saw the flash of their eyes rolling back.

My elbows and knees were pinned down, nails gouging into my neck. I tried to roll, to get free, but my assailant held on. Pain sang across my scalp as my head was pressed into the nubs of teeth beneath me.

My name was shouted from somewhere behind me – not Gabo's name, but my own – and in the next moment the creature was barrelled off as Pablo threw it aside. He held a shattered door in his hands, and swung at a shadowy blur attacking Marquez.

Another creature leapt on me, wrapping its tail – or a vine – around my neck. I twisted, swinging the blade wildly. I tore at the claws – no, the hand – that was pulling the vine tighter and my scrabbling fingers caught on another vine, or string, around my attacker's wrist. As it broke I brought the blade up.

There was an awful feeling of the blade catching, then tearing. The pressure on my chest suddenly vanished. I tasted blood in my mouth, but it was not mine.

I sat up, ready to leap to my feet, but instead saw a thin trail of dark red leading away across the square. Pablo was doubled up and panting nearby. The Governor wiped his blade in the dust. Marquez's other eye was swelling, his clothes ripped to shreds.

The ambush was over as quickly as it had begun. The ringing in my ears faded slowly, the locket pressing hard against my chest.

'Any losses, Marquez?' said Governor Adori.

'All accounted for, Governor.'

The cook was standing by the snapped tether of his vanished horse, saying fast and loud, 'My chickens. My chickens. My chickens.'

I spun around, heart sinking. The bay mare was gone, Miss La's cage nowhere to be seen.

'What were they?' said Marquez, spitting on to the dust. 'The Banished?'

The Governor looked around the village, casting about for clues. 'Can we be sure they were men, not animals?'

'They came at us so fast,' Cook said, eyes wide.

'They had the upper hand,' mused Governor Adori. 'Why did they retreat?'

Pablo held out his hand and as I reached up something dropped from my fist. I looked down, and felt the air leave my lungs.

'Isabella?' said Pablo softly, but I would not, could not, look at him. I was staring at what was lying on the dusty ground strewn with blood and teeth. A lump the size of the locket rose in my throat.

'What's that?' said Pablo. He crouched down and picked it up.

On his broad palm lay a thin bracelet, its ends ragged where I had pulled it free. Twisted in with the threads was a single shimmering line of gold.

'It's Lupe's.'

'What?'

'It's Lupe's,' I repeated. 'I made it for her birthday.'

'Are you sure?' croaked Pablo.

'Yes,' I said, forcing my eyes to meet his. 'I made it. I tied it on her wrist.'

'How did you get it?'

A vine around my neck, my own nails scratching to get free.

'Runts. We need to get moving,' said Marquez, crossing to us.

The others had already untied the rest of the horses. One more was missing aside from mine and Cook's.

'Gabo found something,' said Pablo.

'What is it?' said Marquez.

I tried to stop my voice shaking. 'The bracelet.'

Marquez looked down. 'This?'

He pushed it off Pablo's palm and scuffed the string into the dust with his boot.

'Don't!' I cried. 'It's Lupe's!'

'Lupe's?' The Governor's voice carried across the square. Even the sea, cresting out of sight beyond the broken homes, seemed to fall silent.

'This scrap,' said Marquez, kicking the bracelet towards Governor Adori. 'The boy seems to think it belongs to your daughter.'

The Governor did not speak for a long moment. He crouched down beside the bracelet. I could hear him breathing. His head bowed, he gently ran his finger along the length of string, its gold thread glinting. 'It does?'

'Sir?' said Marquez.

'How are you sure it is hers?' The Governor glanced sharply at me.

'I – my sister made it for her.'

'Isabella?'

I tried not to blink. 'For her birthday.'

'How did you get it?' said Marquez.

'One of them was wearing it.'

Governor Adori stood up abruptly. 'We have to follow them.'

'Sir, we don't even know where or what they are.'

'They're cowards. Taking a child—'

'If it was the Banished, we need to stay away from them.'

'They have my daughter.'

'Sir, I don't think she's—' started Marquez.

Suddenly Adori's blade was drawn, pressed to Marquez's neck. I gasped and beside me Pablo took a small step back.

'There's no body, Marquez. So I suggest you don't finish that thought.' He pressed harder. 'Do I make myself clear?'

Marquez nodded. Governor Adori swung around. 'Good. Any more questions?' Nobody spoke. His eyes were wild. 'Everyone saddle up.'

'Sir,' said Pablo hesitantly. 'They took some of the horses. The cook's, Gabo's.'

'Those without horses make your way back. Except the map-boy.' Adori glanced at me. 'We need you.'

I heard him as though from a great height as I put Lupe's bracelet in my pocket. The locket hung heavy around my neck and I pressed it to my chest through my tunic.

I could not let calling her 'rotten' be the last thing I said to her. I had been wrong about her being a coward. I wanted to tell her she was brave. I wanted to tell her I wished I was as brave.

The expedition shrank to seven. Those with bloodied clothes discarded them for fresh. The Governor had to lend Marquez a set of his royal-blue trousers and tunic.

'Who shall we call Governor now?' joked Jorge, the laugh dying in his throat at the look on Adori's face.

We saddled the remaining horses. I climbed up behind Pablo, too shy to put my arms around his waist until he made me.

After twisting to watch the village of bones fade from sight, I pulled my map materials out and continued marking the distance.

'You don't have to do that,' said Pablo gently. 'You should rest.'

I ignored him. I did have to do this. The quill seemed the only solid thing in the world.

Please, Lupe. Be all right.

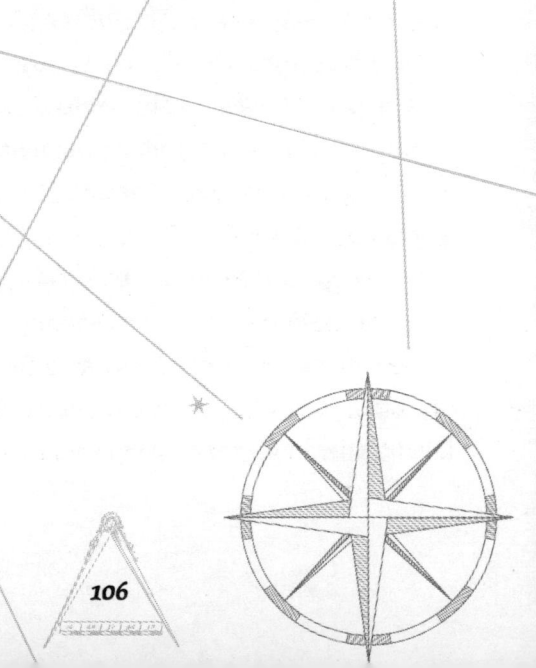

CHAPTER
TWELVE

*W*here would you want to go next, Da? When the ports open again?

If, Isa! If they opened, I'd want to go to Amrica first, of course, but then India.

Why?

India is a place where colour is doubly bright. Pinks that scald your eyes, blues you could drown in.

That doesn't sound so good.

Oh, but it is! The richness, the texture. Just think of the pigment! My maps would be the envy of the world. India is where I would go. Through Afrik, to buy incense to perfume the papyrus bought from Æygpt. You?

I'd come with you, to India. I'd help you find pigments to make maps beautiful enough for queens.

But that wasn't true. I'd wanted to explore Joya, to fill in the blankness at the heart of our island. I'd lied.

And here I was. I looked around, at the blackly swaying

trees and broad sweep of beach, at this place I'd imagined so often, a place that used to feel as distant and magical as India did to Da. But now my body was aching and Lupe's bracelet was broken in my pocket. At least Da wasn't here. With his bad leg he would never have been able to cope with the constant riding, or fight the attackers as I had.

Or, said a quieter voice, *perhaps he could have.* Perhaps I was being unfair, and too kind to myself. Perhaps it was just selfish, wanting to come on this expedition. Perhaps it was just stupid.

A shadow fell across my neck again, but I knew I would find no one behind me. Without my braid my head felt softer, less protected. I leant against Pablo's back.

It all had to be linked somehow. Not just Cata, but also the animals in the bay, fleeing just like the songbirds. The destroyed village. The attack. The connections must be there, but they were fine as spider's silk, glinting in the corners of my mind.

The landscape shifted subtly hour by hour, deserted village by deserted village, and by midday on the third day the world seemed a changed place. The haze had lifted and a fierce sun was beating on our backs. The land had risen up from the sea, so a cliff fell away to our left, and the water was throwing itself against the rocks so hard that flecks of surf hit my cheeks, driven by strong gusts that sacrificed Marquez's hat to the waves.

The Governor did not talk except to order us to rest for a few hours each night, all of us sleeping badly with the wind howling through the dark. His shoulders were hunched, and I wondered if he felt the same weight in his chest, the same tightness in his throat.

The locket hung heavy around my neck, but I would not take it off. I could not, not until we found Lupe. The wind whipped the horses' manes and my eyes stung and watered, the afternoon sun sending light splintering.

Soon we were moving through overgrown fields, obviously abandoned. We must be getting close to the next village, which was just as well. The sun was approaching the horizon, and the constant battle with the wind was exhausting for us as well as the horses.

Fierce sea winds blow from the Frozen Circle around Carment, Da had explained, tracing the path of the wind on Ma's map. *Crops grow horizontal and it is said the Carments are low to the ground too, as if bowed by air currents. We are all of us products of our surroundings. Each of us carries the map of our lives on our skin, in the way we walk, even in the way we grow.*

Finally, the shapes at the top of the slope resolved themselves into buildings. Not the stooped irregularity of ruins, but standing houses.

'Sir,' I said hesitantly. 'The tracks loop around.'

'He's right,' said Marquez. The tracks skirted the outer boundary of the abandoned Carment village, then turned and in an almost straight line backtracked to the far-off forest, further down the slope.

I surveyed the smudge of the treeline. Icy fear trickled

down my spine. What if they were watching right now?

'I think it's best if we stop here, sir,' said Marquez, before the Governor could interrupt. 'The men are tired, the horses need to rest.'

'What do you suggest?' snapped Governor Adori.

'It is better to establish that this village is secure, set up a watch, and pursue them at first light,' said Marquez, lowering his voice so I had to strain to hear. 'I don't trust our chances in the forest.'

The Governor grunted and turned towards me. 'Boy, where do those tracks go?'

I checked Ma's map, though I knew there were hardly any details at the centre. 'The Marisma, sir.'

'Just the swamp? No villages?'

'None on this map, sir.'

The Governor punched his hand into a wall, cracking the mud. I flinched, and Pablo took a step towards us, but the Governor only gave out more orders and strode away.

We tied the horses to a trough. Pablo stayed behind to feed them while we entered the silent village. I travelled at the centre of the group, hand clasped around the blade's hilt, but nothing happened. No one was there but us.

Carment was not at all what I expected. It looked a lot like Gromera in reverse, sloping up towards the coast instead of down. Even the doors were hinged on the other side from ours. Some of the houses were as large as Pablo's and mine put together, with dark wooden doors.

I wiped a thick matting of cobwebs off one. It was

engraved with what appeared to be the dip and swirl of waves. I swept away more, and a large ship complete with sails emerged in profile across the centre of the door. The sails had remnants of red paint flaking off them.

I stood back and tried to imagine the whole surface painted. The blue of the waves, the red-sailed ship cresting on white foam. It was beautiful.

My insides ached for home, with its peeling green door and map-covered walls, and Da. I turned away and wiped my eyes quickly as Marquez prowled past.

I followed him up the slope against the wind. We passed more carved doors, more houses with walls flaking colours, until we reached a large blank space, like a market square except it was curved, the houses set along its edge like an audience. Beyond was the cliff edge. The sea wind here was colder than anything I had ever felt before, and I pulled Gabo's jacket tightly around me.

Far below, the sea whorled and smashed the rocks, rolling unbroken as far I could see. Da said that somewhere far that way was the Frozen Circle, where the bears were white and breath fell in icicles from your nose.

Directly beneath me was a harbour, protected by a stone wall. Any boats it had once held were gone. A thin line of stone steps was carved into the cliff leading down to the bay and, without thinking, I began to descend, clenching the carved handholds until my knuckles paled. The wind died down as I passed into the shelter of the rock wall, and I jumped the last three steps, landing on fine-grained sand.

This sand was as white as Gromera's was black, shining strangely.

I pulled off Gabo's boots and rolled up the bottoms of the trousers. The soles of my feet were a mess of blisters, my heel rubbed raw.

I looked up at the high, dark stretch of cliff to check I was not being watched, but I doubted anyone had even noticed I was gone. Bracing myself, I stepped forward into the shallows.

The water stung like tiny insects, but soon my toes numbed. I was in the sea, with the man who had banned it only a cliff face away. I closed my eyes. I wanted to swim, but even though Ma had taught me and Gabo how in a small lake near the mines, I could not quite dare myself to.

Da said that the Governor banned swimming to stop anyone trying to escape.

Not that they'd get far. The current is changeable and the ocean is full of terrors – jellyfish, sharks, sea snakes.

Why are people so sad to leave the ocean then, Da?

Because it's also full of wonders, and can take you anywhere in this world.

'Anywhere in this world,' I whispered to the locket. 'You hear that Lupe? There are so many places we have to see.'

A muffled *thump* came from behind me. Before I could turn, hands seized my waist. I was being lifted.

I kicked out, twisting and squirming desperately, but the hands were firm and the person was running, carrying me out towards the waves.

Pablo was laughing. He paused thigh high, holding me out above the water.

'Take a breath!'

And with that he threw me into the sea.

My body eased through the slight tug of the current. I had forgotten the sensation of weightlessness, remembered Gabo laughing as he managed to half-lift Ma in the lake. Swimming in the sea was different though. The water was black beneath me, and after a while I scared myself imagining what was below and had to get out.

Rubbing my arms to get warm, I watched the shadow of Pablo, his head slick as a seal's. Just as my legs began to dry he waded out and flopped down next to me.

As if picking up a conversation we had just been having, he said, 'This is even stranger than I thought it would be.'

'Me too,' I said, and he snorted.

'Well, yes, you're the strangest thing out here.'

'You know what I meant.' I felt my cheeks flushing. 'Don't laugh at me!'

'I'm sorry.' He sounded sincere. 'I used to get laughed at, you know. For playing with you and Gabo.'

'Why?'

'You were younger. They used to call me an idiot.'

'Who did?'

'The boys my age,' he said, sifting sand through his

fingers. 'An idiot. Simple.'

'That's not very inventive.'

He gave a soft laugh. 'I suppose not.'

I shot him a sideways glance. 'Is that why you stopped? Visiting us?'

Pablo went very still. 'I'm sorry. For not coming when Gabo . . .'

I felt a familiar closing in my throat. 'It's fine.'

'Are you all right? With all this—' His hand made a short movement towards mine and then he stopped, resting it on his lap again. 'You must be scared.'

'I'm not.'

'I am.'

Another silence.

'Do you think we'll find her?' I said. 'Lupe.'

'Yes,' said Pablo, too swiftly, too certainly, but a rush of warmth pushed through me. I traced the line of the bracelet through my damp pocket.

'Good.'

We sat watching the stars shine palely in the sky. I tried to read them, not like Masha would, for fate, but how Da would, for direction. The North Star held its place firmly above us, not the brightest in the sky but the stillest. Da always called it an anchor, a tethered star about which the sky turned.

'That piece of wood, the one that glows.' Pablo's voice made me jump. 'It's from your da's walking stick, isn't it?'

I nodded, guiltily realizing I had almost forgotten the

Governor had it.

'Do you really not know where it comes from? Why it glows?'

'Not why it glows. But it's from a boat. My great-great-grandfather's boat.'

'A boat? What happened?'

'Pablo,' I said teasingly, 'do you want me to tell you a story?'

'No,' he huffed, lying back on the sand. There was a brief silence. 'Maybe.'

I lay next to him, eyes fixed on the North Star. Da's voice came to me, strong and deep, and I spoke the words the way he would, the way he had so many times on a clear, starred night like this night.

The wood is all that's left of Great-Great-Grandfather Riosse's boat. It was built from a single, special tree, as light, pound for pound, as egret's bone. But this was not the most remarkable thing. When he scratched at the wood, the bark under his fingernails shone. Once cut, planks revealed the glowing grain. Nails slid easily into the wood without splitting it, and when in place held fast. The boat grew beneath his fingers as simply as if the tree had re-rooted itself and taken on a new form. Two months later Luna Flotante *– Floating Moon – was finished, its sides glazed with dragon-tree sap so that when night fell it*

glowed like a beacon of fire. Fish were so attracted by the light that he could simply scoop them out of the ocean with his hands. But his luck did not last.

One night, a strong wind took him too far out. A black cloud rolled in from the far-off coast of Afrik and settled above him. Rain came down like whiplashes, and the boat threw itself about on the crashing water, the wind lifting it up. He tied himself to the mast but it broke. He was tossed into the sea as the boat crested an enormous wave but did not plummet back down. Instead, it was pulled above the storm-riven ocean like a bizarre bird. Then he was dragged under. He knew that death was coming; his lungs strained and his head filled with bright stars of pain.

But he did not die.

The mast bore him to the surface, and held him there until the storm faded. He was rescued by a passing vessel. The crew were bemused by his gabbling. There had been no storm that they had seen, and certainly no flying boat. The only proof was the mast tied to his body.

I can see you are doubting me, Isa, but I believe it. I believe that that boat was not of this earth, or, at least, was not of the human earth. It was given to him by the island, and taken back. All things have a cycle, Isabella, a habit of returning the way they came. Seasons, water, lives, perhaps even trees. You don't always need a map to find your path back. Though often it helps. Now, what do you believe?

CHAPTER
THIRTEEN

I hadn't meant to say the last part out loud, but Pablo did not tease me. His hand slid into mine and squeezed gently, warm and rough.

'Come on,' he said. 'We should get back.'

I picked up the satchel and boots, following him barefoot up the steep stone steps. The wind set about howling again. When we reached the top there were lights and voices coming from one of the larger houses, and outside a fire burnt, protected from the wind by the high wall. A lone figure sat there.

Pablo and I started towards the house, but as we neared the open door the Governor's voice growled from beside the fire.

'Come here, boy.'

I tensed. He had not looked up from the flames, but was indicating a spot next to him. We started towards him but he clicked his fingers at Pablo. 'Not you.'

'You all right?' Pablo murmured.

'Hurry up,' barked Adori.

Shivering slightly, I walked over to him. Pablo paused in the doorway, then went inside.

'Been swimming?' He gripped my wrist, pulling me down before I could answer. 'Sit.'

There was a long silence before he spoke again.

'So this is Carment.' He swigged from his hip flask. I could smell the honey brandy from here, thick and sweet. 'Home of the Banished, some say. Did you know the girl? The dead one?'

'Her name was Cata.' I said, careful to keep my voice flat. 'Yes. She was friends with my sister.'

'Your sister had an interesting assortment of friends,' remarked the Governor.

'She has, sir.' My hand gripped the satchel so tight my knuckles clicked. I wished Pablo had not gone inside.

'Tell me, boy, do you enjoy your work?'

'Yes.'

'You are fortunate, then. My father was a governor, too. Of a town in Afrik. I learnt to fight, helping him to defend it. That is all being a governor is, really. Fighting. My father died trying to defend his power.'

'I'm sorry.'

'Don't be sorry. I killed him, after all.'

His words hit like a stone, and I tried not to flinch.

'But I got my punishment. I'm here, aren't I?' He laughed hollowly and drank again from the flask. *Now*, I thought, *I should ask him now.*

'Why are you here, sir? For punishment?'

'For punishment. For redemption. Failed on that count. Yes. I was sent.'

Redemption? I didn't know this word. I hesitated, then asked, 'Sent by who?'

He was silent a long time, and I wished I was brave enough to look at his face, to judge if I had gone too far.

'You have asked your question,' he said suddenly. 'Now I have one for you. Why do you have my daughter's locket around your neck?'

I reached up. The locket was sitting over the tunic in plain sight. I scrabbled about for an answer, heartbeat loud in my ears.

'Don't bother lying,' said the Governor. His eyes were dull and dark as coals.

'She gave it to my sister,' I said finally.

The Governor nodded for me to continue. It took a few seconds to find where to start, and eventually I settled on Lupe sending Cata to look for dragon fruit, and ending with the letter. I missed out disguising myself as Gabo.

The Governor listened silently. Finally, he spoke. 'Do you believe in fate?'

'Yes. No. Maybe,' I said.

'Give me an answer, boy.'

'My da says it's a word used by people who don't want to take responsibility for their own lives.'

Governor Adori chuckled, a low rumble that held about

as much warmth as Marquez's eyes. 'Does your da talk to you about his childhood? About growing up, and why he became a cartographer?'

'Yes.'

'I don't understand why men tell their children such things,' he sneered. 'It's weak. It's deathbed talk.'

I didn't know what to say to this. I couldn't tell him I thought Da was the strongest person I knew.

'Do you want it back?' I said. 'The locket?'

He blinked at the fire. 'It was Lupe's. It was hers to give, and I doubt she has a use for it now.'

There it was. He thought she was gone. *You're wrong.*

I wanted to shout, to scream at him for giving up on her, but I only bit my lip and hated myself for it.

'Still, I'll have revenge.' His eyes glinted. 'It's what governors do.' He laughed so suddenly I jumped, knocking his arm. He looked down at the dark material of his cloak, at the darker stain spreading from the spilt hip flask. I held my breath.

'Governor?' Marquez emerged from the house. The Governor turned to look at him and waved him forward.

'Take this,' Governor Adori said, throwing his cloak at me. 'That stain needs to be out by tomorrow.'

I took it and stumbled away. As I passed Marquez he gripped my arm.

'I'm watching you, boy.'

I reached the house and stood pressed against the inside wall. I felt as though I'd escaped a forest fire with only singes. Pablo gave me a worried look but I closed my eyes so tightly they buzzed.

Do you believe in fate?

He'd killed his father. If I had not been sure of his cruelty before, I could be sure of it now. I could not let down my guard around him. And Lupe – he thought she was dead. I let that settle heavily on me. I had to believe twice as hard that she wasn't.

'Why do you have his cloak?' My eyes snapped open. Pablo was standing very close. I peered past him into a large one-roomed building with high windows. The others were playing cards around the glowing shard of Da's walking stick. No one had looked up.

'Isa, are you all right?'

'Don't call me that,' I snapped, pushing past him. 'I have to work.'

He frowned but I ignored him. The conversation with the Governor had knotted my insides. I flung the cloak to one side. I would not do anything for that man. Lupe deserved so much better than a murderer for a father.

I wanted home, and maps were as close as I could get to it now Miss La was gone. I spread the materials out in a corner, turning my back on Pablo. The star charts had dried, but were torn and smudged. They were useless. *Sorry, Da.* I looked out at the slice of sky through the window high above me. The North Star glinted back. If I could anchor its position . . .

I began to draw, imagining our journey backwards from

where I sat. I traced the route along the beach, the ground sloping down. I drew the spidery estuary of the river, then the long, slow curve of the beach to Gris, with its X of blood and teeth, marking the treeline and our route all the way to Arintan. Finally my lines met those I had drawn on our first day in the Forgotten Territories, when this all felt exciting as well as scary. When I felt as adventurous as Arinta, sitting beside her waterfall, heart still full of hope that we would find Lupe, and seeing Ma's map reveal its secret paths to me.

I pulled out the ancient map and ran a finger over its surface.

'Please,' I whispered. 'Change.'

But the map only rustled mockingly, ordinary as ever. I rolled it back up and put my mess of a new map away too. It was not like Da's. I was stupid for thinking it would be. I looked at it and saw scale, landscape, landmarks, but no sense of the island I had longed to see. It sat dead on the ground, simply ink on paper. Da's maps always felt alive. Like they were made of more. Ink, paper, and something else, something living.

But there was no point trying to make it better now. Not with my head so heavy, my eyes so tired. I rested my head on the satchel and pulled the cloak up around my chin to stop the draught. As the men played cards and swapped jokes, I dreamt of long-ago murdered fathers and living maps that shifted like sand beneath my fingers.

'Isabella.' Pablo's voice, close to my ear. 'Can you hear that?'

I sat up, listening. I could. A low whistle, just audible above the wind. I peered into the shadows.

'Where's the Governor?' said Jorge blearily.

'Let's go find him,' hissed one of the others.

'Not you two, you'll get in the way,' said Marquez as Pablo and I stood.

'I can help,' said Pablo, drawing out his small knife.

Marquez snorted. 'Not with that you can't. Take this.' He drew a second sword from his belt.

Pablo took it, and shook his head at me. 'Stay here. I'll come back as soon as I know what's happening.'

I nodded as the men drew their swords and left silently, lifting their feet. The door closed. I was suddenly alone.

The wood-light was still on the table, and I tucked it into my belt as I strained my ears, listening for another whistle, but none came. I did not know whether to relax or worry. A few minutes dragged by, and still all I could hear was the wind.

Then came the unmistakable sound of a man shouting out in pain: one guttural note that died almost instantly. My skin prickled.

I drew Da's blade. I did not want to sit and wait to find out what was happening. I put on the Governor's dark cloak to conceal the wood-light's glow, and pushed the door ajar.

It creaked loudly. The curved expanse was empty, the black sea swirling beyond. The fire where Adori and I had sat was out.

A sudden scuffling came from behind the house. Trying to breathe as quietly as possible, I crept towards it, rounding a corner. I clapped my hand over my mouth to stifle a cry.

Marquez was lying there, eyes glassy and sightless. His hands were tied in front of him, but his chest was still rising and falling. He was alive – but where was his attacker?

I had to find Pablo. I shrank back into the shadows, running on as silently as I could. My foot caught on something and I almost fell.

Panic chased up my insides. It was another one of the Governor's men, unconscious and tied.

A rustling noise came from behind me and I ducked, thoughts racing. I had the blade and the wood-light, my satchel. I could get on a horse and go, follow the coast until I hit the ridge and had to take to the forest. I could make it home.

No, said another, more insistent voice. I should try to find Pablo. I could not leave like this. Arinta would not. I straightened and turned back to the square.

A smell like burning ships filled my head, then my hands were being wrenched behind me.

I kicked out and opened my mouth to scream but a bitter substance was forced in, dissolving on my tongue. My gums went numb, blood running cold.

The world slipped away as thick smog clouded my limbs. Dust filled my mouth as I fell forward into blackness.

CHAPTER
FOURTEEN

Everything hurt. Everything felt weighted, pinned down. The wood-light was digging into the base of my spine, satchel squashed beneath me. I pulled it out and cracked my lids open.

I gripped the wood-light until I felt solid again, tried to sit up, head throbbing viciously.

A dark, worried face swam into sight. I squinted until it came into focus, then clamped my eyes shut. Shock ratcheted through me in cold waves. I was dead, I must be.

But I didn't feel dead. I could feel the ground, feel the pulse in my neck.

I peered up again. The thick halo of black curls was clumped and matted, the face dirtier than Señora Adori would ever allow, but there she was.

'Lupe?'

'I knew it was you! Even with your hair all gone.'

I threw my aching arms around her, pressing my face

into her musty curls. Lupe squeezed back, so hard I felt my shoulders pop. She was shaking, and I could feel the nubs of her spine against my forearms.

'Are you all right?' I whispered.

She sat back on her heels and rubbed her face.

'Better now you're here. Why are you wearing Papa's cloak?'

'It's a long story.'

Lupe let out a hiccuping laugh and drew her legs up to her chin. 'I bet.'

Her skirts rustled – she was still dressed in pink taffeta, though now it was muddy and torn around the hem. Trust Lupe not to have changed out of her birthday dress before leaving for the Forgotten Territories.

'We thought you were dead.' I could not keep the wonder out of my voice.

'I thought I might be too.'

'What happened?'

'It's a long story.' She had dark hollows under her eyes. 'Doce found me.'

'Doce?'

'She's a governor's daughter too, sort of. Her mother, Ana, is leader of the Banished—'

'The Banished?' My skin crawled.

'They found me, in one of the villages. Grit, or something.'

'Gris.' This did not make sense, that she was here and alive and dressed in her best clothes, talking about the Banished.

'Lupe, we need to get away from here. The Banished killed Cata.'

'No,' said Lupe. 'It was something else that killed her.'

My heart hammered in my ears. 'What?'

'Can we wait until Doce gets here? She explains much better than me. Anyway, I was in Grit—'

'Gris.'

'—because my horse bolted and I couldn't stop it, and it was running towards the sea but Doce stopped it. I fell off and landed right on some bones. Did you see them?'

'Yes, I saw. What happened there?'

Lupe's eyes went wide as plates. 'The air killed them. That's what Doce said. Something floated from the ground and made it hard to breathe. Like poison.'

'Poisoned air?' I couldn't stop staring at her. 'But I found your bracelet . . .'

'Where?'

I took it out of my pocket. 'I pulled it off someone. Someone who attacked me.'

Realization dawned on Lupe's muddy face as she took it. 'Oh, it was you! They were just trying to get the chickens. The animals are all gone you see.' Lupe shuddered. 'It sounds awful. They all ran into the sea.'

The chickens. That's why the attackers had left as soon as they had seized the horses with the chicken cages.

'Doce made stew. Except for this one chicken, it was all mangy and grumpy so they let me keep it. Like a pet, you know.'

She pointed to a pen in the shadows and I scuttled over. It couldn't be – and yet it was: Miss La, pecking irritably at some seeds. I made to pick her up but she squawked and snapped her beak. She was obviously not as happy to see me as I was her.

'Do you know each other?' Lupe frowned.

I nodded but did not explain. It felt too long a story. I looked about, noticing for the first time the stakes beaten into the ground in a circle around us, stretching high into the branches above. A cage, surrounded by black forest. The ground was soft, not packed hard and dusty like in Gromera, and the air smelt of stale water, though I could not see any.

I checked the satchel, pulling out Ma's map. This must be the Marisma, the swamp at the centre of the island. I traced the route to Gromera. If we could escape the cage, we could get home. I placed it carefully back in the bag, along with the wood-light.

'You don't mind about the bracelet, do you? I gave it to Doce to say thank you for saving me from the Tibicenas.'

I frowned. 'Tibi-what?'

Lupe shivered. 'I . . . I'd rather not talk about them right now.'

I could not decide if I was dead after all, or dreaming. Nothing Lupe was saying made sense. Lupe being here, saying anything at all, did not make sense. She was frowning at me.

'Isabella, are we still friends?'

I took her hand. 'Of course we are.'

'You don't think I'm rotten?' She looked on the verge of tears.

My stomach twisted with guilt. 'No. I'm sorry I said those things.'

She nodded. 'That's all right.'

I picked up the bracelet, and tied it back around her wrist. 'Have you seen your father yet?'

'My father?' Lupe frowned. 'Why is he here?'

'We came to rescue you. You didn't think I got here on my own, did you?'

'He came to rescue me?' Lupe tilted her head, bird-like with her nest of knotted curls. 'My father?'

'Yes. And me and Pablo and some of his men.'

Lupe's lip wobbled. 'He brought all those people in order to find me?'

'Yes,' I said, impatience growing. 'We need to get out of here. We need to find them.'

Lupe's eyes caught on something behind me.

I turned slowly. For a moment there was nothing. Then a girl stepped forward into the clearing through an entrance concealed in the circle of stakes, emerging as if the air itself had parted and formed her.

The Banished girl came closer. Her movements were fluid, her body and dark clothes smeared with mud except for a relatively clean stretch of cloth bound around her arm.

My mouth went dry as I remembered bringing my blade up in Gris, the feeling of resistance . . . had I done that?

I could not bring myself to meet her eye, flinching as she held something towards me.

'You need to drink,' said the girl, thrusting out a clay pot. 'It's boiled. It's safe.'

My mouth was parched. The pot was heavier than she had made it seem. I gulped the water down, barely pausing for breath. It tasted strange, like earth.

'She says my father was with her, Doce. Is he here?' asked Lupe.

Doce nodded. 'You ask too many questions.'

'And Pablo?' I said, stomach full of water. 'Is he here?'

'I don't know their names.'

'A boy. He's tall, like a man, but he's wearing a white tunic.'

'They were all in uniform. Blue, with gold stitching. We're keeping them over there.' She gestured vaguely into the darkness. I noticed her accent was not smooth like Lupe's or mine. Her words were full of flicks and clicks, her tongue clacking.

'What's going to happen to them?' asked Lupe.

Doce didn't answer.

I could guess it was nothing good.

'So no boy in a white tunic?'

'No.'

One of the small knots in my chest slipped open. Pablo had escaped.

Doce must have mistaken my expression for something else, because she said, 'I'm sorry. I'm sure your friend will be all right.'

She did not sound convincing.

'All right? Why wouldn't he be?' All the dangers seemed accounted for. The Banished were obviously the ones who had attacked us in Gris.

Doce looked towards Lupe. 'You haven't told her? About...'

'I have. I just couldn't tell her what.'

I waited for someone to explain. 'Tell me what?'

'About the Tibicenas.' Lupe's voice was lowered. I remembered all over again: Cata.

'What are the Tibicenas?'

Doce sucked in a long breath, and the staccato in her tone grew more pronounced. 'They came from below, ten days ago. They killed that girl in your village, nearly killed Lupe, too. One had her cornered in Gris when we found her. We killed it, made the cross out of its teeth to warn others off. But creatures like that, they don't have souls. They don't get scared.'

'It was awful.' Lupe's voice was tiny. 'It was the biggest thing I've ever seen. All drooly and so black it was like...'

'Like it sucked all the light out of the world,' finished Doce.

'But what are they?' I said, impatient.

'They're demon dogs.'

Demon dogs. My mind whirred. 'Like in the myth of Arinta?'

'They're like huge wolves. We thought that's what they

were, at first,' said Doce.

'Well, there were wolves on the island.' I hoped I sounded like Da would if he were told this – calm, reasonable. 'They used to live in the forests. Then they moved to the caves—'

'They're not like those sorts of wolves. They're . . . they're bigger than wolves,' Lupe insisted. 'And black as soot, with eyes red as fire.'

I looked to Doce for guidance, but she only nodded solemnly and said, 'My mother says they're Yote's. They're his fire dogs, his Tibicenas. They've been sent to clear the island.'

I felt stupid but all I could do was repeat her words and hope they made more sense in my mouth. 'Clear the island?'

'Before Yote takes it. That's why the animals left. They feel Yote first. Well, first after the island. You must have noticed the trees?'

'Yes, but—'

'But you can offer a better explanation? For trees that look like they live off ash, for the water drying up, for the animals fleeing?' Doce's voice was tight as a tripwire.

I shook my head. 'If this is true—'

'It is.'

'—what are you going to do?'

'Escape to the sea, like the animals.' Doce's eyes were wide in the gloom. 'We're leaving today.'

'Where are we going?' Lupe piped up.

'Gromera, first,' Doce said. 'We're going to take the ship.'

'My father's ship?'

My voice was unsteady. 'It won't work.'

'What?'

'The ship—'

But before I could explain about the burning, a strange clicking started.

It seemed to be coming from everywhere at once, a sound that could have been far-off rain or the chirruping of insects but for Doce's reaction to it. She bolted upright, away from us, and began clicking her tongue. Miss La squawked, scrabbling around her pen and I lifted her up to try and quieten her.

It grew louder and louder, and I sensed something surrounding the clearing. The clicking stopped. Doce bowed her head slightly. 'Mother.'

I squinted towards the trees Doce was addressing, but could see nothing until the woman was nearly within touching distance.

She, too, was small, strong-looking, dressed in mud and dark cloth, holding a staff. Her weather-beaten face was lined but quite like her daughter's. Except for the eyes. There was no gentleness there. Even Miss La stopped struggling under her gaze. A scared child would irritate this woman rather than soften her. I stared back.

She took another step forward. Suddenly we were surrounded, as dozens more mud-clad figures entered the cage or climbed the branches to peer down at us.

Lupe had gone rigid beside me but I did not take my eyes

off Doce's mother. The woman began to circle, her back slightly rounded, her stride shortened by a limp. I saw a deep indent on her right calf, as if someone had scooped the flesh from it.

When the woman spoke her voice was clear and loud as a bell. 'We have a set now. What are you? The Governor's son?'

'His servant.' I said, willing myself to sound unafraid.

'Why do you wear his cloak?'

'She's a girl, Mother,' said Doce.

'Oh,' said Ana, in a tone that showed it would take more than a girl in trousers to shock her. 'Why do you serve a dog?'

I shifted uncomfortably, hoping Lupe was in her usual state of not paying attention. 'I had no choice.'

'Just as those who were banished had no choice? Just as the man who did this—' she turned her back, lifting her tunic, and Lupe made a retching sound – 'had no choice?'

Her shoulders were a mess of scars, criss-crossing in raised ridges as if a tree were sending its roots through her back. Ana rolled her shoulders, and a crack issued from her spine as the movement sent a spasm across the scar tissue. I stroked Miss La's soft feathers, trying to calm myself.

'There is always a choice. Now we have to decide what to do with your master.' She turned to Lupe. 'Your father.'

The crowd parted and a small group of men in Governor's blue were shoved into the cage. No Pablo. I counted them quickly. One, two, three, four, five. Only five? I strained to see their faces. One was in dark-blue Governor's robes . . . Marquez, wearing Adori's spare set.

Lupe was frowning at the men. 'My father? My father isn't—'

'Lupe!' interrupted Marquez. 'My child!'

Lupe opened and closed her mouth like a fish. 'I – I don't—'

The other men caught on.

'Governor,' said one. 'The journey was hard. It has taken its toll on all of us.'

'Yes, sir,' said another hurriedly. 'Do not be upset if your daughter does not recognize you.'

I did not think they could risk being much more obvious, but Lupe still did not seem to get what was going on.

'I am not surprised your daughter chooses not to know you,' snapped Ana. 'I would be ashamed to have such a father.'

'Marquez, stop.'

Governor Adori stepped through the open door. No one moved for a long moment. I felt my pulse thrumming in my wrists.

The silence broke as Lupe leapt up. 'Papa!'

Ana hissed and stepped between them, clenched around her staff.

'Stay there, Lupe,' said the Governor.

Lupe was nudged roughly back to the ground beside me. She started shaking again, and I passed Miss La to her.

'Don't let them see you're afraid,' I whispered. She held

the chicken tightly to her chest.

Marquez dropped his head, defeated. 'Sir, I would have gladly—'

'It is not your place, Marquez.'

'It is not your place to call yourself *Governor*.' Ana put mocking emphasis on the last word as she stalked up to him. 'I know why you came. You had a chance to redeem yourself, and you failed.'

She kicked his legs out from under him and he went down hard. Ana clicked her tongue and his hands were tied tightly behind him.

'Then I will pay,' said Adori, struggling to his knees. 'But let my daughter and companions go.'

Ana chuckled joylessly. 'I will do better than that. I will take them with us when we leave.'

'You are leaving? Why?'

The tension between them was taut as a storm cloud.

'You know why,' Ana spat. 'Because there is a deeper darkness here, a darkness we cannot defeat. I care more for my people's safety than for revenge. That is the true mark of a leader.'

The Banished clicked their tongues, like a ripple of applause.

'What deeper darkness?' Marquez said, raising an eyebrow.

Ana fixed her eyes on the man and strode towards him. 'One that will shake that smirk off your face and swallow the ground from under your feet. Yote is coming.'

He snorted. 'That old wives' tale? That superstition?'

'Is it superstition that drove the animals into the sea? Is it superstition that murdered one of ours? If I'm not much mistaken,' snapped Doce's mother, 'that superstition is what brought your *Governor* here in the first place.'

She faced the Governor again. 'Now we must get moving.' She whistled and the men were hauled to their feet.

Doce led us to them. Lupe hugged her father tightly as soon as Ana's back was turned.

'We don't have time for this now,' said Adori, shrugging off Lupe's arms. 'You must be brave, Lupe.'

He turned his exhausted gaze on me. 'I believe you have something of my daughter's?'

The locket. I took it off and Lupe held out her hand. 'How did you know Isabella had it?'

'Isabella?' The Governor looked at me long and hard. 'Of course.'

The secret lifted off my shoulders, but I tensed, waiting for some punishment for deceiving him. It did not come. He seemed unable to focus on anything but his daughter.

'Put the locket on, Lupe. Don't give it away again. It is a part of our history. A piece of our story.'

CHAPTER
FIFTEEN

I wrapped Miss La in the Governor's cloak to stop her thrashing, and we settled into formation, prisoners at the centre of the long procession. Ana seemed to know the way, and from the stars I could tell we were heading south through the Marisma, directly towards Gromera.

I tried not to think of the half-finished map in my satchel, the half-seen island being left behind, and forced myself to focus on each step taking me closer to Da. Whatever welcome met us in Gromera, I would find a way to get him out of the Dédalo.

In the darkness it was hard to tell how many Banished there were. Fifty at least, with cloth bags and vine nets of possessions lashed to their backs. All believing Yote was real, believing there was a ship in Gromera's harbour, ready to take them away. How would they react to a border thick with guards, the ship burnt in the harbour? The Governor's men had not told them, and though I was not sure whose side I was on I did not want to draw attention by telling them myself.

Lupe did not speak, whereas usually I could not get her to shut up. She was carrying herself rigidly, eyes fixed on her father's broad back. I put my free arm around her.

'Why does he not speak to me?' she said, her voice barely a whisper. 'I . . .' She sniffed and squeezed her eyes shut. 'I thought things might have changed.'

I did not have an answer.

The night was hauntingly clear. The stars revealed their places in constellations and the moon's pull felt physical on my short hair. Something was happening to the very air we walked through. It was tense, alive and threatening, the island in the grip of forces shifting imperceptibly beneath my feet.

All night the wind chased us, the mud sucking like fingers. In the dark it was difficult to tell the unsafe, bog-like mud from water, or the water from land, but I took care to watch for the slight ripples or softening that meant we were on dangerous ground.

My feet began to ache. I thought of Pablo, out there in the black forests with the wolves Doce called Tibicenas. I thought of Cata. Miss La cocked her head up at me and pecked at my chin.

As the hours passed and our pace slowed, my thoughts became oddly detached. My stomach hurt and snatches of Da's stories and Ma's face and Gabo's sing-song voice danced across my senses, disorientating and magnetic.

'Are you all right?' Doce asked, as I almost stumbled over a root.

'Mmm.' I didn't trust myself to speak.

'Here.' Doce passed Lupe and me something. 'It's dandelion root. It will help to wake you up.'

It was tough to chew and tasted bitter, but after a while I felt the tiredness lift, the world come back into sharper focus. I blinked in the pale morning light and realized we were walking alongside a dried riverbed.

I fumbled in the satchel for the map. It was battered and torn, creased as my tunic, but still legible. On this side of the island, the river could only be the Arintara. Ahead stretched the last of the swamp.

Once we skirted it, we would reach Arintan, and soon after that I would be home. And Da—

'Ouch!' I'd walked straight into the man in front. He shushed me urgently.

Adori turned to Doce. 'What's happening?'

The Banished girl had frozen, the muscles in her legs tensed as if ready to run. 'Don't you hear that?'

I listened, rubbing my shin. I could hear nothing except the black trees rustling, but the other Banished were as tense as Doce, scanning the trees to our right. Slow as a whisper, the adult Banished slid forward, forming a line facing the forest, weapons drawn. Miss La woke with a loud squawk and began scrabbling frantically at the cloak.

I clenched her firmly under my arm, feeling the dandelion root sending sparks through my blood, the energy turning to fear with every passing moment. All was still for several long seconds, then came a noise unlike anything I had ever heard before.

Loud and rumbling, lined with a hard, metallic edge that set my teeth chattering. A roar. It flew towards us, flooding through the trees.

My skin prickled, a thin acidity filling my throat. Somewhere inside me, something was weakening, coming apart. I wanted to run, but couldn't.

Beside me, Lupe was clutching her stomach. 'It's them!' she moaned. 'Do you feel them?'

'They drive you out of yourself,' said Doce. 'The Tibicenas.'

'But they're not real,' said the Governor. His tied hands trembled. 'They can't be.'

'You know about them, Papa?'

But he did not answer Lupe's question. Doce spun around, raised her blade and cut the vine tying the Governor's hands. 'Run. Take them. Cross the swamp, straight through, it'll be quicker. Follow the river, and run.'

The Governor took Doce's arm in a vice-like grip, his fingers sinking into her skin. 'I will stay.'

Ana was suddenly beside us. She wrenched his hand off Doce's arm. 'Don't touch my daughter!'

'I'm telling her I will stay and fight with you.'

'Papa?' said Lupe, uncertainly.

Ana arched her eyebrow.

'It's my island too,' he hissed. 'Whether you like it or not,

I will defend it.'

They regarded each other like two dogs circling before a fight. Then Ana took a blade from her belt and handed it to him.

Another howl rent the air. I cringed, insides churning.

'How will we know how to get home, Papa?' cried Lupe.

'I know the way,' I said, slipping my hand into hers.

'Run! That's an order!'

Behind us, Adori sliced Marquez and the other prisoners free. I expected them to run, but instead they accepted more swords from Ana and joined the line of Banished facing the forest. Some of the younger Banished were already fleeing.

The noise came a third time through the dawn light. My stomach twisted again. 'We can stay, we could help!'

'Papa, I don't want to go without you,' Lupe pleaded. 'Please come with us, Papa—'

But Adori only swept her into a tight embrace, and said fiercely, 'Go, run fast, Lupe. And remember the locket.'

Lupe's face was wretched. 'You said not to open it until—'

Adori took the ring of keys from his belt and pressed them into her hand. 'You have to go now.'

He nodded at me. His hands had stopped trembling. 'Take care of her, Isabella.'

He pushed us away just as another roar cut through the trees, followed by a collective yell from the Banished. I spun around to see them lifting their weapons like a thicket, Adori and Ana at the front, side by side as something monstrous broke through the treeline.

High as a horse, covered in black, matted fur. It moved on paws thick as tree trunks, flicking its terrible, deep-red eyes left and right.

It was no wolf. It could only be a demon dog. A Tibicena.

It landed a few metres from the line of Banished with a sound like a thunderclap. Its claws scraped the ground, leaving deep gouges in the dust. More howling came from the trees behind. More were coming.

The Governor, Ana and Marquez stood together. The other Governor's men were bunched around them, blades drawn.

My churning insides brought white points of pain to my eyes. The beast's presence seemed to be pushing my insides out and away, as if my body were water being whipped up by a storm. No wonder the animals had fled to the sea, if this is what they'd experienced. I felt like a songbird caught in the sharp gaze of a raven, tiny against the darkness closing in.

Lupe was tugging on my hand, screaming for us to run. Heart wrenching in my breathless chest, I turned away just as the creature lifted its massive paw.

I did not see it fall.

CHAPTER
SIXTEEN

We ran across the swamp, hands clasped, and I remembered the last time we had run together, through the fields to school. I could feel Miss La shaking. Soon we reached an area that was more water than land, trees lacing through the swamp and vines hanging down, dangling into the Marisma like snakes.

'We have to swim,' I said, tying the cloak into a sling around my back with the chicken pressed against my neck. We launched ourselves into the thick water, churning our legs.

I felt myself sink, Gabo's boots filling with water and slipping from my feet. I kicked hard, unable to find ground or to float in the liquid mud. I splashed upwards and felt Miss La flapping angrily.

'Sorry,' I spluttered, grasping a vine and manoeuvring her up higher, out of the water. I lashed myself to the vine and shouted for Lupe to do the same. Other shapes were around us, other children fleeing.

I wrapped my fingers around another vine a few inches in front, levering my foot against a root to gain purchase in the sucking black. We pushed ourselves forward, reaching for a vine an arm's length ahead. Together we repeated the movement, finding something like a rhythm.

Time seemed to compress and lengthen with my body. I could hear only Miss La's worried clucks and the laboured sloshing of our movements, see only the black water and looping vines. It was as if we'd fallen below the earth, where stars could not shine and all around us was the underworld. I tried not to think of the scene we had left behind, wondered where the other fleeing Banished had disappeared to.

Eventually the vines thinned. Our feet scraped along mud thick enough to walk on without being sucked under. We were nearing the opposite bank. This thought propelled me forward and soon I was pulling myself up, hands raw from the fibrous thorns of the vines. Beside me Lupe was picking them from her sopping skirt. She looked dazed.

'The swamp will buy us time,' I said. 'Come on.'

But with the next step, the ground dropped away. We tripped and skidded down a dip, bowl-like and pitted with fallen, rotting fruit that turned to pulp beneath my feet. The smell was overpoweringly strong and sweet.

My heart raced as I lifted my foot. Something had

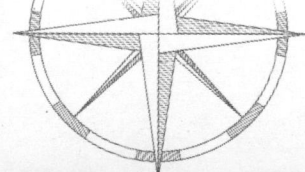

wedged itself between my big and second toe.

'What – what is it?' Lupe's eyes were wide as plates again. I pulled it out and Lupe cried out.

A bone, small and still lined with gristle. We had found the Tibicenas' feeding pit.

I swallowed back vomit as the rot filled my nostrils. Lupe was already scrambling ahead, but I was rooted in the putrid earth. *Don't panic*, I told myself.

Go.

Clambering on all fours up the other side of the pit, through the decomposing flesh, through jawbones and femurs, I held my breath until I stood once more on the damp ground.

Lupe had stopped a few metres ahead, and through the trees we saw a slow, rippling shine. A silver thread leading home.

'The Arintara,' I said.

We paddled in the trickle to clean the dried blood from our feet, and I let Miss La out to run in circles in the shallows. Lupe took my hand.

'I'm sorry,' she croaked. 'For leaving you behind just then.'

I squeezed back. 'It's not your fault.'

'You don't think I'm rotten?'

'No,' I said firmly. 'You're brave. You came into the Forgotten Territories when no one else would. Not me, not my da, not—'

'Not my father.' She took a deep, shaking breath.

'My father . . .'

I thought again of the matted paws, the bones in the feeding pit, then gently unfurled Lupe's clenched hand. The set of keys was embedded into her palm and I peeled them out, sliding a needle-thin key off the ring.

Lupe looked from the key to me, and back again.

'He never let anyone touch them, not even Mama. Why would he give them to me?'

I gave the needle key to Lupe.

'Papa said not to open the locket until he died.'

I took her hand.

She stared down at the key as though she had never seen anything like it before.

'He's dead, isn't he?'

I nodded. Lupe nodded too, slowly, as if she was trying force the fact into her brain. Her face was oddly blank.

Lupe took off the locket and slotted the key into the lock. There was a faint click, and it sprang open. Out came a surprising amount of water, and then a sodden piece of paper, folded into a square that fitted neatly inside.

Lupe was about to unfold it but I touched her hand lightly to tell her to be careful. The water would have made the paper fragile. Lupe passed it to me, her own hands shaking. I peeled it open. It had been folded many times, and the paper was so thin I felt sure it would rip.

Eventually, I spread the letter out on Lupe's lap. The ink had bled slightly around the edges but the words were clear. I read the first lines before I could help it.

My daughter,
If you are reading this, then I am no longer with you. I wrote this so that you could know all the things I could not bring myself to tell you when living

I caught myself, and turned to look at Lupe. Her mouth was pressed into a thin line, and her eyes were so sad I looked away again, fiddling with the remaining keys.

Minutes passed. Everything seemed quiet and still, except Lupe's light breathing and the slight twitch in her gangly leg. I waited as she turned the paper over to read the other side. After another minute or so, she let out a long sigh, her body going slack.

Then she carefully folded the paper, picked up the locket and put the letter back inside. She closed it and threw it with all her might into the river.

'What are you doing?'

'I don't want it.' Tears were dripping from her chin. I reached out to comfort her, but she moved away.

'What . . . what did it say?'

'That my father is everything the Banished said he was.' Her voice was strangely dispassionate. 'And worse.'

'Lupe, I'm so sorry he died . . .'

She looked at me. Her face was not sad any more, but angry.

'I'm not.'

I did not know what I was about to say, but just then we heard a sloshing sound, something disturbing the water upstream. I didn't feel the pain in my stomach that I'd felt when a Tibicena had approached, but still I grabbed Miss La and we left the riverbank, ducking behind the treeline. I gripped Lupe tightly as a large shape came into view.

It took me a moment to realize. Then I was up and running again, sending the hen spiralling.

CHAPTER
SEVENTEEN

The next instant I was hugging Pablo so tightly I heard the breath whoosh out of him.

'Isabella? What—'

'You're here! How?' The relief flooding my body felt like eating all the dandelion root in the world.

'Don't sound so disappointed,' he said, returning the hug so awkwardly I felt my cheeks flush and I stepped back. 'But how are you here? I saw you taken by the Banished. I tried to follow but I lost you in the dark.' His voice had a husky tone to it. 'I thought I wouldn't see you again.'

He looked around, catching sight of Lupe. She was standing by the riverbank. I could not read her expression.

'Is that the Adori girl?' said Pablo. 'Where's Adori?'

'He stayed behind with the Banished,' I said carefully, aware that Lupe could hear us. 'To fight.'

'Fight what?'

'The Tibicenas. What they call demon dogs.'

Pablo's eyebrows disappeared beneath his fringe. 'Demon dogs? Like in the myth?'

I nodded.

'I see.' Pablo's tone was mocking. He caught sight of Miss La splashing around on the bank like a suffocating fish and again raised his eyebrows. 'What is happening here?'

'We don't have time for this,' Lupe exclaimed impatiently.

'She's right,' I said. 'We have to get to Gromera.'

'Agreed,' said Pablo. 'If we follow the river—'

'Isa knows,' interrupted Lupe. 'She's been directing us fine so far.'

She picked up Miss La, who sat docile in the crook of her arm, and began striding down the river.

'What's wrong with her?' Pablo jerked his head at her retreating back.

'She's been through a lot,' I said, wondering what the letter had said. Pablo fell into step beside me.

'What really happened?'

I told him about waking up at the Banished camp, about Ana, and Marquez trying to take the Governor's place.

'So Adori was there? I saw him running away when the men got attacked.'

'Well, he came back.'

'Unlike me, you mean?' Pablo said sharply. 'I did try to follow, but they took the horses and—'

I shook my head. 'I'm not saying that. I'm saying he tried to make it right. When the Tibicenas attacked . . . what's so funny?'

'That you can even say that word with a straight face—'

'They are real!'

'What did they look like?'

I tried to explain.

'Sounds like a wolf to me.'

'It's the way they make you feel. Doce says—'

'Doce?'

'One of the Banished – Ana's daughter. She says they drive you outside yourself. You feel them coming. Your insides go funny, like a storm in your stomach.'

'What's that meant to mean?' said Pablo, smirking. '"Storm in your stomach"? Sounds like what happens after eating your da's cooking.'

'You wouldn't be laughing if you'd been there,' I said, flatly. I suddenly felt exhausted. I didn't want to think about it. I just wanted to get home and see Da. Not even my half-finished map made me want to stay in the Forbidden Territories any more.

'You tired?' His face was kinder now. I shook my head even as I yawned. 'You sure? I could carry you for a bit.'

I looked at him sharply in case he was teasing, but he was holding out his arms. Attaching the Governor's keys to my belt, I checked Lupe was not watching, then hesitantly wrapped my arms around his neck. He lifted me and under the smell of sweat and blood there was lavender again, fainter than ever.

Breathing it in, I listened to the rhythmic sloshing of his feet. I could not believe he was here. And Lupe was ahead, chattering away to Miss La. If I let myself forget what lay behind, it almost felt all right. Almost.

I closed my eyes and floated on a deep, black ocean that sparkled and shone, reflecting a clear night sky full of stars. Across the water came a boat made of glowing wood, so light it barely skimmed the sea's surface. As the boat approached I saw swirling carvings on its sides, and in the shallow hull stood my family. Not just Da, but Ma and Gabo too. All three were pale as moonlight, and glowed with an aura as wondrous as the vessel they sailed in. Gabo stretched out his fingers and, as the dream-night shone around us, I took his hand.

'Isabella, look!'

I blinked blearily into the midday glare. 'What is it?'

I felt suddenly awake. Ahead, the ground seemed to drop away into nothing. Except I knew it was not nothing – it was Arintan. We were coming to the edge of the ridge the expedition had followed on its outward journey.

Pablo set me down, steadying me as the blood prickled back into my legs. 'Nearly home,' he said.

I walked to the edge of the waterfall and peered over. 'It's a long drop.'

Lupe looked too, then passed Miss La to me and without pausing scrambled halfway down the rocks. She tucked her skirts up and jumped lightly down, landing with a quiet splash. I gaped at her as she climbed back up simple as a cat, barely panting. 'Not so bad.'

'Show off,' mumbled Pablo.

It was as I turned to tell him off that I felt it: the pushing away, my insides twisting. Pablo's face creased and he held his stomach. 'What is that?'

'Oh, no,' said Lupe frantically. 'Oh, no, no, no!'

'Run!' I shouted, just as a huge shape materialized behind Pablo.

But there was no time. Pablo turned to see the Tibicena, its hackles raised along its spine, the slash of its mouth opening into a booming roar, like a thousand rocks smashing down a cliff.

'Help me!' I yelled, heaving at a boulder by the waterfall's edge.

Pablo lifted it, waiting until the creature was within range and then hurling it easy as a skimmed pebble. It hit the Tibicena hard, trapping its leg.

'Go!' I shoved Lupe towards the lip of the ridge and threw a squawking Miss La to her as she landed at the bottom.

I chanced a look back. The Tibicena had freed itself but seemed to be struggling to stand, its back leg hanging oddly. Pablo grabbed my arms and half pushed me over, crouching on the slippery surface to lower me.

Then I was falling the last few metres, landing on the soft mud of the riverbed next to Lupe. Pablo splashed down beside us, sounding like Gabo falling into the clay mine. For one, wonderful heartbeat I thought we had done it, had escaped.

But then the Tibicena loomed over the ledge, readying itself to jump.

Pablo urged us forward. 'The path's over there. Run!'

I sloshed after him but Lupe stumbled, going down hard against the rocky side of the waterfall. Miss La was off and scrabbling to the trees. I wrenched my arm from Pablo's grip and ran to try to help Lupe to her feet, but she was a dead weight in my arms, her terrified eyes fixed on the dark shape above us.

Pablo's momentum had carried him further downstream, and he spun around to come back for Lupe and me. Too late. I felt the Tibicena's shadow thunder over like a wave as the creature threw its broken body down between us, reeling around to face the waterfall. To face Lupe and me.

Pablo searched for a weapon. He picked up a stone and threw it at the Tibicena's flank but it only glanced off the matted fur.

'Go!' I shouted desperately as Lupe and I backed away. 'You have to warn Gromera!'

The Tibicena drew back its lips in a snarl, black saliva stringing down to the ground.

Pablo's face was set. 'I'm not leaving you!'

He grabbed a pointed stick from a pile of branches – the firewood we had helped collect only days before – and jabbed it hard into the Tibicena's injured leg. The beast roared as it rounded on Pablo, lifting an enormous paw. Its claws slashed through the air, catching Pablo across the face.

I saw his eyes go blank, and he fell back against the riverbank, motionless. Blood blossomed across the water towards me. Pablo's blood.

The Tibicena reared as if to strike again. I began to scream.

I screamed Pablo's name, I screamed at the Tibicena to stay away from him, and Lupe screamed with me. He was not dead. He could not be dead.

We started throwing slick pebbles from the riverbed and splashing our feet, trying to get the Tibicena to leave Pablo, to turn towards us.

It worked.

Lupe and I fell silent, our breath coming in tight gasps. The Tibicena was preparing to attack, taking its time. Beyond it I saw Miss La's tracks in the dusty ground by the trees, but for Lupe and me, there was nowhere left to go.

I took one last look at Pablo. Was that movement in his chest? A rise and fall, barely a whisper, rippling his white tunic?

'Isa,' squeaked Lupe. 'Now what?'

I pulled her backwards blindly, through the thin stream of water and into the cave. We backed right up inside the large chamber I had reached on my first visit to Arintan. I felt the horizontal striations of the rocks against my back, and tried to summon Gabo as the Tibicena appeared at the mouth of the cave.

The smell was rot and rage and sweat. My insides wrenched and turned. I wanted it over. Lupe found my hand.

It sprang, and Lupe pulled me down. I heard the rush of air as the Tibicena launched itself at us. I cringed, bracing myself for its weight to crush us, for its claws to rip into us—

But it never came.

There was an ear-splitting *crack!* as the rocks behind me gave way. The force of its leap had carried the Tibicena straight through the wall, and a few seconds later we heard a sickening crunch.

Hollow. The back of the waterfall was hollow.

We crouched, frozen to the spot.

'Are you all right?' I croaked.

'Never better.' Lupe's voice was high and small.

I hiccuped out a short laugh. My belly and ribs ached and I felt dizzier than ever as I looked around.

'We should go.' Lupe's face was graver than I had ever seen it. 'Pablo.'

I shuddered, remembering how still he had been, his barely-there breath. Cold spiked through my chest.

I took Lupe's outstretched hand and pushed against the shattered wall to stand up.

A mistake.

A grinding sound rose through the silence. The base of the wall gave way behind me. As I lost my balance, I tried to let go of Lupe's hand, but she held fast.

Together, we plummeted into dark.

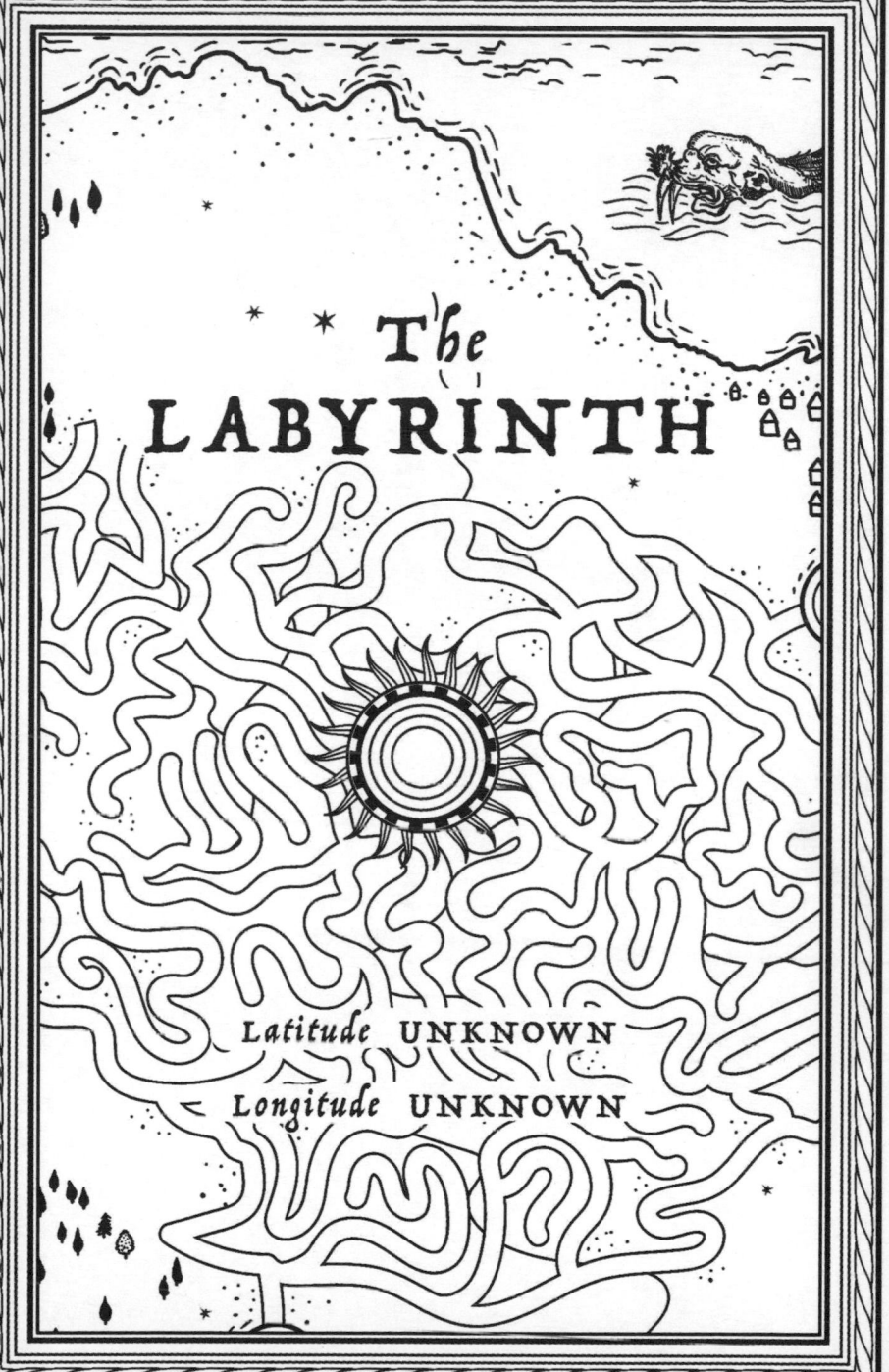

The
LABYRINTH

Latitude UNKNOWN

Longitude UNKNOWN

CHAPTER
EIGHTEEN

an you stand at the point you are at, in any room —
your room, say — and accurately remember it?
Could you walk outside into the yard and make me
a drawing of it in the dirt? It's only a small, simple room.
You've lived there ever since you could walk. Two beds,
probably a sleeping cat on one, a chest full of clothes.

What about scale? We can't draw it the size it is, even a
small room like that. We need to scale it down. Would you
give me a matchbox bed under a tiger cat? Could you
remember the size of everything in relation to everything
else? This relationship is more and more important the
larger we go. A tree in its place in a forest, an island
tethered in the sea. In Ma's map, the only one we have of
the Forgotten Territories, each kind of tree is marked. The
detail matters. Even in mapping your bedroom.

Landmarks next. A circle for rest and comfort: the cat
and the bed. An X for danger where the loose nail sticks out

of the chest. A snaking line for the voice line between your bed and Gabo's.

Perhaps this is it. This simple square, marked in the dirt. This is a map you could go and buy from any map-maker, anywhere in the world. If they'd seen the room, this is what they would give you. An accurate measure of itself. But could it show the feel of the place?

This is what a cartographer does. We make the maps come alive. Your room would have the quality of home. You would look at it, and know it not as a room, but as your room, where you have spent your childhood. And we can make maps of places we were years ago. Here, on Joya, I could make you a map of Afrik that would have you breathing the incense of the markets until you were dizzy with it. My map of the Frozen Circle could have you reaching for fur socks and running from a white bear! Well, almost . . .

That's a way off for you, little one. But this is a start! You have drawn your first map. Write your name across the top. Here, you can use my peacock quill.

I-S-A-B-E-L-L-A.

Perfect.

I shifted. Dark rushed in, along with the echo of my own heavy breathing.

Crack!

Something broke close to my ear. I tried to move, but Lupe had landed across my leg and arm. She was unconscious, chest rising shallowly.

Crack!

This time, something broke beneath me. I put my free hand out and a wave of nausea rippled through me as thick, stinking fur met my fingertips. That noise . . . the ribs of the Tibicena were giving way beneath our weight.

With a final glut of cracking, I heaved Lupe off and scuttled away from the two shadows until I hit a damp wall of rock. The last moments before our fall were coming back: Pablo trying to save us, being struck down. His blood spreading through the water.

I closed my eyes.

'When I count to ten,' I murmured to the blackness, 'everything will be all right. One, two, three . . .'

But by 'ten' the world was still as cloaked as ever. The satchel was pressing into my back. I pulled it out and felt inside for the wood-light. Its glow dispelled the darkness and I looked over at Lupe, who groaned and sat up gingerly.

'Are you all right?'

She opened her mouth to reply and blood spilt down her chin.

'You're hurt!' I gasped.

'Ith's fine. I bith my tongue.' She stuck it out for me to see.

The bite wasn't deep. I gave her a gulp of water, and she

swilled it around her mouth, spitting out red.

'What happened?'

'We fell.' I pointed up to where the gap was, at least five metres above us, rock dust still streaming down.

'We fell all that way? And nothing's broken?'

I shook my head. 'You can thank our friend.'

Lupe followed my gaze and yelped, dragging herself away from the broken body of the Tibicena, tar-like blood still leaking from its muzzle.

'Ugh! It's . . . it is dead?'

If it wasn't before we landed on it, it was now. Lupe did not seem to want to get any closer to it than I did, letting out a long breath. I looked up towards the hole from which we had fallen. It was barely visible.

Lupe craned her neck. 'Do you think we can climb it?'

I ran my hands over the rock wall. The rock was slimy and crumbled at my touch. My fingers came away damp.

'We can try.'

There were no hand-holds to speak of, so I tried emptying the satchel, climbing on to Lupe's shoulders and throwing it, hoping for the strap to hook the ledge. It did not get close. We piled the rocks from the collapsed wall on top of each other, and this time Lupe climbed on to my shoulders, stretching towards the gap, but even without my shaking knees it was still an impossible distance away. All the time we called for Pablo, but there was no answer. I tried not to think what that meant, even though I knew he would come if he could.

Lupe sank to the floor, burying her head in her hands. For a moment it sounded like she was laughing, but then the gulps resolved into stifled sobs. I reached out to help her up but she shrugged me off. Her nose was running.

I slid down the rough surface of the rock wall and sat on the damp ground next to her, repacking the satchel as I faced the thick darkness of what I was sure was a tunnel. If it was, I could not ignore how we had found it.

Through the waterfall. Just like Arinta did, on her way to fight Yote.

Think.

Doce said the Tibicenas came from below – this tunnel, and others like it, must be what she meant. The Tibicenas could not be reaching the surface from here. We had only just broken through the back of the waterfall's cavern and there was no way up. That meant there must be other exits.

Lupe quietened, her breathing still irregular. I stood and helped her to her feet.

'We're going.' I pointed into the darkness.

Lupe shrank in on herself, shaking her head. 'No, I can't . . . I hate the dark.'

'We have to.'

'I don't have to do anything.'

'There must be a way out.' I said, more certainly than I felt.

'But you don't know that!'

'We'll make it, we will. I . . .' I trailed off.

Lupe glared. 'What? You promise? You don't know the way out. You don't even know there *is* a way out.'

'The Tibicenas had to come from somewhere. The Banished said they came from below.'

Lupe glanced over quickly to where the wood-light illuminated the slack shadow, then at the tunnel mouth. 'Maybe the horse boy will wake up soon. If we just wait . . .'

I didn't know what to say. I could not tell her what she wanted to hear, and could not say why I did not think Pablo would come. I could not think he was—

Stop thinking it, then.

But I also could not stay here and wait to die, any more than Lupe could stomach entering the darkness. If only I had a map, I'd feel safer facing the unfathomable black ahead.

'A map!' I gasped as I remembered: Ma's map changing, the lines appearing and vanishing as I watched. The satchel floating in the Arintara . . .

'What are you doing?' Lupe asked as I emptied the satchel on to the floor, inks and ripped star charts tumbling.

The map was at the very bottom. I unrolled it and smoothed it out on the damp ground, holding the wood-light over it.

'What's—' started Lupe.

'Shhhh!' I stared hard at the paper, but nothing happened. I sat back on my heels, rubbing my eyes with frustration. Then—

'Look!' Lupe was pointing at the map.

It was changing. The trees and villages were retreating,

sucked into the surface, a new landscape developing slowly.

'Why is it doing that?'

'The water . . .' My heart was thumping too hard, too loud. 'It was the wrong water.'

'What?'

I wished she would be quiet. It was clear now. The first time the map had changed, it had been drenched by the river. The river at Arintan. When I tried to recreate the change, I used water from the flask filled at home. Now the ground was again damp from the waterfall. The map had to be wetted with water from Arintan to reveal this hidden layer.

I snatched the map up and waved it around. As the corners began to dry the original images reappeared.

I held the map against the dripping rock wall. The lines regrew and intersected, covering the outline of Joya in a mesh of what I now realized were tunnels. Dotted across the network were circles. One was positioned above the place where the waterfall had just faded. My breath caught. The circles were exits. *Thank you, Ma.*

'What is it?'

I looked up, smiling broadly.

'It's our way out.'

I measured the distance to the next exit with my fingers. We would have to walk miles along the tunnel to it. I was not happy about venturing so close to the red circle that crouched at the centre of the map, but we had no choice.

I did not tell Lupe what I thought this circle meant. If she didn't want to go into the dark, I didn't think mentioning a fire demon would be much comfort. I had never hoped so hard I was wrong. For now, our only concern was getting out of the maze. Even the black forest would be a comfort. Anything above ground would do.

We drank from the rivulets trickling down the wall. The water was grainy but it tasted fresh enough. We drained our flasks of their stale water and refilled them. I soaked the map through and we set off, the way illuminated by the wood-light.

It was difficult to keep track of how long we walked, each step reverberating off the walls, the heat growing all the time. I tracked our location by moving my finger along the lines on the map, tracing our progress from corner to corner, bend to bend.

It took all my concentration, so I did not speak except to direct us left, right, straight ahead, or to ask Lupe to dampen the map. The air stank.

Lupe wrinkled her nose. 'Smells like off fireworks.'

Whatever it was stung my lungs, leaving a bitter taste on my tongue, but I could not waste water washing the feeling away. The downward slope of the ground increased minute by minute, and soon we were sliding down a steep channel. I hoped it would not take us too deep.

Da's stories spiralled through my mind, one joining up

to the next. But it was the myth of Arinta that returned again and again. *She entered through a tunnel behind a waterfall.* I cast a sideways glance at Lupe, wondering if she had been listening any of the many times I told her the story. But her face was set in a grimace, pulse going fast in her temple.

As we scrambled further into the depths of the island, the heat intensified. Sweat ran down my face, steam lifting off the map as it dried. Soon Lupe had emptied one of the flasks of half of its water.

We reached a crossroads, four tunnels intersecting. I squinted at the mesh of lines, trying to work out which one we should take, but they vanished.

'It's drying out too fast.'

Lupe groaned in frustration. 'We can't use the water like this, we need to keep some to drink.'

'I'll try to sketch the route,' I reached into the satchel for the map-making materials. My hand closed on nothing but the blade, and my half-finished map. Along with the keys and water flask on my belt, they were all I had. With a sinking heart I remembered emptying the bag, the pile of inks and paper stacked where we had fallen with the Tibicena.

'I left everything behind. I'm sorry—'

Lupe made a hushing sound, 'Shhh!'

'I said I'm sorry,' I sulked.

'No, seriously, Isabella.' She held a finger to her lips, taking the wood-light from my hand and burying it in the satchel.

Then I heard it: a shuffling sound, echoing down the tunnel to our right, followed by a low growling. I pulled Lupe into the shadows of the left-hand path just as the pushing away started in my stomach. I felt the walls blindly. They were pitted with cracks and gaps.

A handful of moments scattered as the Tibicena approached, Lupe moaned, creased over, and I dug my fingernails into my palms as we heard it stop at the point where we had just been, sniffing the air. Then it let loose a horrible sound, sharp, with a rattling undertone that shook dust from the tunnel ceiling. I swallowed, tongue sticking to the roof of my mouth.

The seconds dragged by. Eventually, the Tibicena turned and began racing up the slope in the direction we'd just taken. Lupe exhaled in relief, but then the tunnel began to shake. I pulled Lupe into a crevice no wider than Miss La's coop.

We wedged ourselves in, satchel squashed between us, as the Tibicenas came swarming from all directions, panting and returning each other's calls, sniffing the ground. The black shapes blurred past, like a swarm of bats, rousing clouds of stinging dirt, and the bitter smell in the air intensified.

I felt my throat closing, lungs sucking in like sponges. Lupe was stifling coughs into the crook of her arm. A couple of Tibicenas seemed to pause near our hiding place, but were soon swept along by the tide of the pack. Just as

I couldn't stand the pain in my stomach any longer, the shaking stopped. Soon, only echoes and hanging dust remained.

Lupe squeezed out of the crevice again. I followed, relief humming through me, and pulled the wood-light back out of the satchel.

'How long until they reach the waterfall?' Lupe asked shakily.

The Tibicenas moved much faster than us, but it was a steep incline for most of the journey and we must have walked for a couple of hours already. If the Tibicenas did not realize that they were following the scent in the wrong direction . . .

'We might just make it.'

'Which way?'

I held up my hand to look at the map, but it was not there. I opened my fist and a fragment fluttered out, coming to rest on the claw-marked ground.

'No.' I dropped to my hands and knees, scrabbling in the dust near the crevice. The corner must have ripped as we scrambled in.

'Over here.' Lupe's voice was oddly flat.

I raised the wood-light in the direction of her outstretched finger, uncertain what she was pointing at. Then I saw a corner of the map in the dirt. Then another scrap, and another.

It was torn to pieces, pressed like petals into the dust by the stampeding Tibicenas.

'Can you fix it?' Lupe asked, though surely she knew the answer.

I looked into the darkness. It stretched around us, featureless and terrifying.

We were lost.

CHAPTER
NINETEEN

I did not know what to do. We could not stay here now that the Tibicenas had our scent, but we did not know the way, nor what lay ahead.

To my surprise Lupe did not shout or blame me. She knelt and began gathering up the fragments.

'Leave them,' I said quietly. 'There's no point.'

Tears threatened. That was Ma's map, all I had left of her.

Lupe ignored me and collected as many bits of the map as she could. She piled them carefully and held them out. I rubbed my eyes fiercely.

'It's all right to be scared, Isabella,' she said. 'I'm scared, too.'

I looked up, blinking hard. Her expression was soft, and I remembered that face from years before, from the day we first became friends. Lupe holding out her hand as I sat crying by the abandoned rabbit warren, missing Gabo.

I took the fragments.

The satchel's strap had also snapped, so I emptied it, putting the keys and fragments in the pouch on my belt. I kept the blade in my hand, the worn leather of the handle comforting.

'What now?' Lupe asked, suddenly brisk.

I squeezed my eyes shut and again tried to call the map to memory. I knew we were close to where the map had indicated an exit. When I had looked, just before the first Tibicena arrived, where had we been?

The answer bubbled up behind my closed lids. Southeast. Beneath the Arintara. That was it! The tunnel had curved and turned, but had roughly followed the line of the river. What next? The three possible routes onwards.

'Isabella?'

Lupe's voice sent the vision of the map spiralling away. But it didn't matter. I knew.

'We need to take the right passage.'

'Yes, but how are we meant to know which one that is?'

'No, the right-hand passage.' I pointed. 'That one.'

She looked at me doubtfully. 'That's where they came from.'

'They came from everywhere,' I said impatiently. 'That's the way out. We need to follow it to a sort of twisty bit—'

'Twisty bit?'

'Yes, like a knotted rope, but if we stay on the left side of the knot and take the first path off it, we'll get there.'

I was almost sure. Almost.

We continued in silence. The path led downwards. The only good thing about the destruction of the map was now we could use the water for drinking. We passed a wide turn-off scored with paw prints, and I felt Lupe relax slightly as I led us past, into a narrower tunnel that was unmarked.

The heat was growing, and soon I had a throbbing ache drilling deep behind my temple. The sharp smell became stronger, until the air was barely breathable. My head was light and the world around me felt soft and too close. I blinked, trying to push everything back into focus. Lupe seemed dizzy too, stumbling occasionally and dragging her feet.

Worst of all was the sameness of the surroundings. Without a sky, time meant nothing. I measured the distance by the ache in my legs. I longed for the clear skies above Gromera, bright with sun or with stars, even the haze of the Forgotten Territories and the fearful wind of the Carment village.

My knee jarred painfully. The tunnel, suddenly horizontal, curved sharply ahead, and its height dropped by almost a metre. Head bowed, we walked on, the ceiling continuing to slope until we were bent almost double. The Tibicenas would surely have trouble fitting through this space if they tracked us here, but what if I was taking us the wrong way? We would be trapped.

My throat tightened, but we had to keep moving.

The tunnel continued closing in until we were crawling on our bellies, clothes catching on the rough edges of rock.

It would be impossible to turn back in such a small space. I followed closely behind Lupe's feet and tried not to think about the massive weight hanging above us, the whole of Joya poised over our heads.

The tunnel curved again. I guessed we were in what I had called a twisty bit, the tunnel looping back on itself. This passage should intersect with others soon, and then we would take the first left, hopefully to an exit. I drew in a long, steadying breath, the air sharp in my chest.

'Lupe, I think we're going the right way.'

'I hope so,' came her muffled reply as she spoke over her shoulder, 'I don't think I can stand this much longer.'

'Well, no. We can't stand at all.'

'At least you're small!' Lupe's laugh was cut short. Her head and upper body rapidly disappeared, legs slithering after. I reached out, dropping the wood-light in my panic, but was left grasping air.

'Lupe!'

A muted thump from the darkness ahead.

'Lupe?'

Her reply made me jump, sending rock dust streaming.

'I'm all right! It's only a short slope. Isa, you've got to see this . . .'

'What is it?'

'Just lower yourself down. It's safe.'

I inched ahead, feeling for the edge. I dropped the blade and heard it clatter down, then hung for a moment, letting my weight tip me forward.

It was not an elegant landing, and I only just missed the blade. I waited for Lupe to laugh, but she was oddly silent, standing at the centre of a cave, face tilted up. I did not need the wood-light to see her, because its glow bounced back at me from all directions.

A million crystals arced over our heads, throwing out light that danced and shifted, like underground stars. Even the rock beneath my knees glinted below the glittering ceiling.

Da had told Gabo and me about places like this. *I've never seen one, but once I met a man who had found a crystal cave under a river. Some crystals are formed by water, others by fire.*

And as there was no water here, no river . . . it had to be fire.

There are two kinds of crystals. One is granite, a light-coloured rock. And, like you two, it has a twin, a dark version of itself. Its name is 'gabbro'. Gabo, Gabbro.

Now as I stood, surrounded by the walls of glittering crystals, that coincidence came back to me, like a gift.

Something clicked slowly into place, like a sum. It all added up. The smell, the crystals, the heat. I could not ignore it any longer.

'Lupe? I think I know what this is.'

Lupe didn't answer. Her eyes were fixed on the crystals.

I took another deep breath and said, 'It's a fire pit. That's what formed these.'

Fire pits happen where the ground is so hot it melts.

Imagine that, whole lands filled with flame! Sometimes it rises and swallows entire towns. Gabo hadn't liked that, but Da had calmed him. *But more often they sleep and rumble a bit. Or make crystals named like twins.*

I opened my mouth to tell Lupe, but she was looking at me oddly.

'Did you say a fire pit?'

Just like in the myth of Arinta. I recalled Ma's map, how the lines had seemed jumbled but still led to the centre. That strange red circle, at the centre of a map a thousand years old. I took a deep breath of acidic air.

A demon's promise lasts a thousand years.

'What are you thinking?' Lupe's face was wary.

I was thinking of the drought. I was thinking of the Governor's animals, fleeing to the sea. I was thinking of the people in Gris, poisoned by the air.

'The knot on the map was close to the red circle,' I said carefully. 'Maybe only a mile. I think the exit is that way.' I pointed to a tunnel on our left. 'But that way leads to the red circle.' I pointed to another, lower tunnel ahead. It shimmered in a different way from the crystals. It shimmered with heat.

'So?'

I nearly changed my mind. But now was not the time to doubt. 'Yote is in that red circle.'

'Yote?' She wrinkled her nose. 'From that story you like?'

I bristled. 'He's a fire demon. And it's not a story. It's a myth.'

'What's the difference?'

Irritated, I rubbed my eyes, grit grinding against my lids. 'A myth is something that happened so long ago people like to pretend it's not real, even when it is.'

Lupe did not say anything for a long time. When she spoke, it was in a careful, calming voice, as if to a dangerous animal. 'Isabella, Yote is no more real than Arinta.'

'Arinta was real!' My voice echoed around the cave. 'And anyway, what about the Tibicenas? They seemed real when they were chasing us!'

'Maybe the horse boy was right,' she said in a determined voice. 'Maybe they were wolves—'

'Wolves as big as horses, whose fur stinks of smoke?'

'Because they live underground, near a fire pit!'

'They're driven by more than hunger. They didn't eat Cata. They killed her, left her to be found.'

A warning, Doce called it. *They've been sent to clear the island.*

'Don't be stupid, Isabella. You've got to stop believing these things.'

'But Arinta—'

'Is a story! And you're not her!'

Her words hurt but I wasn't about to let her see that. 'I don't think I'm—'

'If you're telling me that is the way out, I'm going. And you're coming with me.'

'You can't tell me what to do!'

'I'm older than you.'

'I don't care.' I snatched the wood-light from her. 'I'm going without you.' Not looking at Lupe I strode towards the passage shimmering with heat.

A sudden pulse shook the ground beneath me. I stumbled and almost fell. Lupe had been brought to her knees.

Another, more violent shudder ran through my body. A single crystal fell from the cave ceiling high above, and shattered between us.

We locked eyes for a moment.

Then the world caved in.

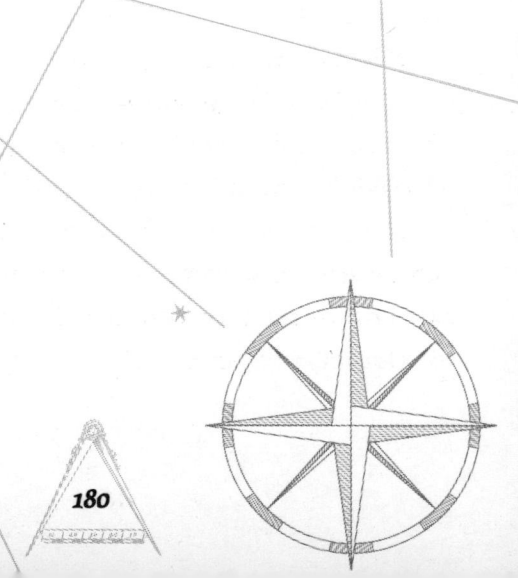

CHAPTER
TWENTY

T he noise was tremendous, like ten thunderstorms and fifty fireworks and a hundred Tibicenas jumbled together.

I ran to the side of the cave, pressing my palms to my ears, but the sound tore through me, forcing me to the ground as if under a giant thumb. I curled up, teeth chattering, head thumping. The ground roiled like the sea, and I waited for the rock to crush us, or to open up beneath me . . .

It did not. With a final smatter of pebbles, the tremors stopped. I opened my eyes, squinting through rock dust. Smashed boulders and crystals lay piled the full length of the cave, dividing it in two.

Lupe was nowhere to be seen. I shouted her name but only an echo came back. I stood up and searched for a way past or over the rock wall, but the boulders were packed solid and my arms shook as I tried to climb them. There was no way out, except the tunnel behind me – the one that led to Yote.

I cowered against the hot wall of the cave. Tiredness covered me like a cloud. I wrapped my arms around my knees, and sobbed.

The cries came echoing back, sounding distant and detached. Eventually I stopped, so I didn't have to listen to myself. But the distant sobbing did not stop. As I listened I thought I could make out a word . . .

Is . . . ella. Isa . . .

It was my name. And that voice – it was Lupe!

I ran my hand over the wall, and found a crack splitting its curved side. I followed it as far as I could reach. Then I pressed my mouth to it and said, 'Lupe?'

I placed my ear back over the crack. Nothing. Even the crying had stopped. Perhaps I had imagined it?

Then a voice, faint and tentative, spoke my name.

Heart singing, I spoke into the same place, 'Find the crack. Speak into it.'

I waited impatiently, ear against the rock, and then Lupe's voice came, as clearly as if she were standing beside me.

'Isabella? Are you there? What's happening?'

Like the crystals, it felt as if Gabo was in this somehow. Chest tight, I replied, 'I'm here. I think it's a voice line.'

'A voice line?'

'Gabo and I had one, in our room. They carry your voice. Something to do with the curve of the cave.'

'What happened?'

'I'm not sure,' I lied, eyes fixed on the tunnel, certain I knew.

'What now? I've tried climbing over the rockfall.'

'Me too. What about the tunnel to the exit?'

'Blocked.'

Clearing my throat, I tried to make my voice strong and calm. 'The way we came into the cave, is it clear?'

The sound of her breathing vanished, and I pictured her moving across the cave to check. A few moments later, her voice trickled into my ear again. 'It's completely blocked. There's a gap near the top, on the side. I think I could move some . . .' She sounded exhausted.

I steeled myself, but Lupe spoke before I could.

'I will try. Then get you across. We'll find a different way, take one of the other paths—'

'Lupe—'

'And then we can get out of here, go home. I'll start now.'

'Lupe, it won't work. I – I think you should go.'

She talked over me, faster and louder, her voice thick.

'I think I can do it.'

'It's all right, Lupe.'

'No, I will, I just need to rest my arms . . .' Her voice trailed off.

'Yes, you should rest. And then you should go back.'

'I'm not going anywhere!' Anger flared in Lupe's tone. 'And you need to promise me the same.'

The low tunnel was emanating heat. I had already

decided what I was going to do. I had decided the moment I saw it. So I lied, yet again. 'I won't go anywhere.'

'Good,' she said. Then, in a more authoritative voice, as if I hadn't already suggested it, 'I think we should rest now. Are you going to sleep?'

'Yes.'

'Isa?'

'Yes?'

'Are you going to stay there, near the voice line I mean?'

'Yes.'

Her fear made things easier and harder at the same time. I lay down, head twisted awkwardly to stay near the voice line, and waited for Lupe to fall asleep.

My stomach rumbled loudly. I ran a hand over it, feeling the hard lines of my ribs, remembering days when I'd frown at our simple meals of bread and whatever fish Da had managed to buy at the market, asking why we didn't eat like people did in his stories of bygone feasts. A meal like that would be a feast to me now.

One of my favourite tales was about the six villages of Joya coming together in Gromera to celebrate the island's six-hundredth year of peace. *This was in the old days,* Da said in his storytelling voice, *even before Arinta. People brought wild boar and roots cooked with ground chillies and vinegar, dates in spun-sugar baskets, palm-sized oysters in pearly shells, crabs and lobsters boiled and served heaped with lemon-scented butter, an octopus the length of a man, shoaled in samphire and salt . . .*

My stomach rumbled again. Lupe's light snores slid down the voice line, pulling me out of the feast and into the dark. I pushed myself to my feet. My head spun and pins and needles tingled up and down my fingers. Swallowing back the sick feeling, I walked five short paces to the low tunnel mouth. I squeezed my eyes shut and let the heat press on my lids.

I stepped forward.

This tunnel was different.

The rock seemed the same kind as in the rest of the maze, but the air was thick with a strange fizz of energy. It sparked up through my feet and made them tingle, as if I walked on a bed of upturned pins, not stone.

The noise grew threatening as I followed the path, the channel narrowing. A now-familiar sensation of claustrophobia began to cloud my mind. I would have given all the stories in the world for one breath of cool, clean air. Before all this, I didn't think I was afraid of anything. Now the dark was only one fear on a long list.

The way the tunnel continued to turn without spitting me back out where I began could only mean that it was coiling, like a shell. The ceiling got lower and lower, until I was forced on to my hands and knees.

Then the sparks started.

At first they were tiny, but as I followed the tightening coils, gaps opened up in the floor of the tunnel, blazing with heat. I put the wood-light in my belt so I could pull myself forward faster. Sparks flew through the cracks, occasionally landing on my clothes. A small flame caught on my sleeve. I fumbled for the water flask and poured a few drops over it.

A wonderful coolness rushed over my skin. Thin bands of blue danced across the fabric where the liquid had landed. I knew it was not normal water – the map's transformation had proved that – but this was something else. I looked at the flask, shaking it slightly. It sloshed, nearly full.

Arinta entered through a tunnel behind a waterfall, drenching herself in the water to protect herself against the flames.

I poured a small amount on to my arm, waited for the blue to spread, and held it out to one of the flames. It licked at my skin harmlessly as a breeze. I crouched and carefully rubbed more water over my skin and clothes, until only parts of my back were left unprotected. When I continued it was as if I was doused in ice.

Da once told me about an iceberg that drifted down from the Frozen Circle when he was six, two decades before the Governor arrived. It came out of the Joyan night like a ghost ship, bumping into Gromera's bay with such force that it gouged a piece of land right out of the earth. It was why Da became fascinated with seeing new places, and with charting them. Because of the ice, he was a cartographer. *It's odd how things are connected.* He always said that. Da did not believe in fate but in each decision affecting the next, like a shout starting a landslide.

How many connections had brought me here? The possibilities made my head spin as the tunnel got lower, the cracks in the floor wider. My hip bones scraped painfully along the uneven surface, knees chafing as the space got smaller and smaller, closing around me . . .

Soon the tunnel was sloping downwards at an impossible angle, and the weight of my body dragged me forward faster than my arms could brace against the sides. The thought came too late that I should have gone feet first. I tried to wriggle around, but could not fold myself without getting stuck.

As I tried to manoeuvre back again my palm hit a loose rock. It was too late to find something solid to hold, though I tried, nails scrabbling for a crack, anything to stop me falling. Finally I managed to wedge my bare foot into a crack, wrenching my ankle. Something gave in the soft pad of my foot and I bit my lip until the throb eased.

Ahead of me the tunnel fell away in an almost vertical slope. I brought my knees up to my chest to lodge myself in place, and craned my neck. At the bottom, it opened out – on to what I could not see – but smoke was billowing up, starting to fill the tunnel. I coughed as a rumbling noise funnelled up with greater ferocity than ever before.

I slip-skidded down to the opening, and gasped, drawing acrid smoke into my lungs. Below me, a gigantic, fiery mouth gaped at the centre of a pit, opening and closing, spitting out molten rock. A fire pit. Ledges ringed the walls, flickering with heat that struck me like a blow.

The skin on my cheeks was blistering, and my insides felt as raw as my skin. My head swam and I heaved myself backwards, cramming my legs across the tunnel to keep from falling, coughing and shaking uncontrollably.

Though it felt like for ever, it could not have been more than a matter of minutes since leaving Lupe in the cave. Yet here I was, wedged inside the very rock of Yote's lair. Like Arinta, a thousand years before.

I thought of all the people I had not been able to say goodbye to. Da, in the thick dark of the Dédalo. Pablo at the riverbank. Lupe, sleeping trustingly above. What would happen to her? Would she survive this?

Enough. I had to get closer to Yote. I may not be Arinta, but I had to try to save Joya.

I lowered myself carefully, so my legs dangled down to the ledge below. It was a long drop. I was about to let go when the shaking started again. But it was not the same as the tremors in the crystal cave or the Tibicenas running. This was deeper, more menacing even than a Tibicena's howl. Just as I tried to pull myself back, my hands slipped, sending me hurtling, feet-first, into the abyss.

My hips hit a ledge with a crunch, breaking my momentum, and I found myself hanging from my forearms. Legs swinging uselessly, kicking out over a searing nothingness, my body shook worse than ever. I clawed at the gritted rock, tearing my nails. It was no use. I did not have the strength to lever myself up.

But now it came to me, strong as a voice in my ear: I did not want to die.

Lupe was right. I was not Arinta. I was not special. I wished Lupe were here now, pulling me up with her long arms. But she was asleep, still trusting my lies. And now I could not even do what I came here to do. I could not save her, nor Da, nor Joya.

My grip gave way. As the ledge shuddered with another violent shake, I fell.

I landed hard on the ledge below, breath knocked viciously from my lungs. My back felt broken in two, white-hot pain sizzling across my legs and the nape of my neck. For a moment – maybe a minute, maybe more – I could not move. My body was full of molten sand, the ground was not beneath me, though I could feel it solidly there.

Liquid blackness behind my eyes, in my ears. Quiet, at last.

Then, bright stars pricked the air as the rumbling tremors grew. I could feel them, a persistent ripple moving as though the earth itself were water, rolling waves around me. I *could* feel them. I was sure. But still there was nothing beneath me, as if I was hovering. Part of my brain was all pain, all noise; the other was nothing, nowhere, not there.

Something was very wrong. Though I was sure I could not, I sat up – didn't I? – I peeled away, coming free, my body dropping behind me like a cloak. I did not look back at it, slack on the ledge. I felt it left there, and the me now crawling to the edge felt rock gritting my knees as I peered over.

Yote hung before me.

He was not the writhing mass of smoke and molten rock that had filled the pit, but a form that was close to human, only huge, emerging from a column of fire that raged beneath his six limbs, spreading from a torso that swirled with ash clouds.

He spoke, in a voice that brought smoke rushing up from beneath him and sent it tumbling around until I choked. The voice rattled and rasped, like the death throes of a Tibicena. But inside me, the me kneeling on the edge of the ledge, a point of pressure opened up near my eye, and from this place I felt his words burrow into my brain.

What do you want?

To stop you, as Arinta did.

My voice was lost, fluttering desperately from one self to another, caught between throats. I was on my knees, I was on my back. But Yote seemed to hear me. Again pressure pinched my skull.

You're too late.

Fingers closed on my shoulders. I shut my eyes, ready to fall.

CHAPTER
TWENTY~TWO

'What are you doing?'

I was rising, my body pulled upwards.

'What the hell do you think you are doing?'

It was Lupe, shouting at me, dragging me, my arm across her shoulders as heat sent the air roiling around us. Cracks were opening in the walls and she squeezed us through, my head knocking on the rock.

Now I could feel the pain, all of it, through my back and shoulders, cutting across my legs, tearing at my head. It did not matter that Ma's map of the Forgotten Territories lay in shreds in my pocket. It was like carrying a map of the journey on my skin, each scrape a path that drew us further on, each bruise a reminder. And Yote's words, burnt into my brain, a line of white-hot beads threaded deep inside.

You're too late.

The ground gave an enormous wrench, and I felt Lupe carrying us forward even as a chasm opened beneath her feet. We curled ourselves into a tight tangle of limbs, and dropped like stones.

I wished for the end to be quick, to smash us against rock, or into fire. But instead we clattered painfully downwards. The labyrinth would not release us. Yote wanted us in the depths of his maze, where no light beyond his could reach.

The rocks grew smooth under my back. A roaring sound filled my ears, like water and fire and wind all mixed up together. But the shaking had stopped. I stopped rolling.

I turned on to my side so I could see Lupe, my head spinning, the wood-light jutting painfully into my hip. We seemed to be in another cave, but this one stretched high, the ceiling out of sight.

'Are you all right?'

'I'm getting used to falling down things.' Her face was pale. 'I wish the ground would stop moving.'

'How did you get to me?'

'I shifted the rocks.' I noticed her hands were covered in cuts, her fingernails shredded, her thin legs scraped. How had she carried me?

'Isa, what happened back there? I thought you were dead.'

'So did I,' I joked, but I could not tell her about the peeling away, the two selves, speaking to Yote. She would not believe me. I did not know if I believed myself. 'I think I must have fainted—'

But I was saved from coming up with an explanation,

because Lupe was no longer paying attention. Her eyes were fixed behind me. 'Isa, turn around.'

She looked as she had in the crystal cave. I followed her gaze, and felt my jaw drop.

Behind me, inches away, a black fire was cascading. A waterfall, a firefall, held in place by an invisible barrier. But the fire was not only travelling down. It was also pushing upwards, outwards, swirling this way and that. As if we had fallen beneath the sea, were watching it churn through glass.

Glass. I crawled forward.

'No!' Lupe shouted. 'What are you doing?'

'It's all right,' I said. 'Watch.'

I pressed the wood-light slowly into the black fire. Lupe gasped as the surface gave slightly, like the skin on milk. Then she pulled herself forward, so that we lay side by side on our bellies. 'This is incredible! What is this stuff?'

'It's glass,' I replied.

'Glass?' She frowned. 'Like the windows in my house?'

'Yes.'

'But how is it here?'

That roaring sound, the sound like the sea.

'It's molten sand. Da—'

'Da told you, of course, but how does it work?'

'It's sand. We must be under a beach. When you melt it, it forms glass. I'm not sure how exactly. This is black because of the bits of shell in the sand.'

'Isn't sand always bits of shell?'

'And other things, like crystals.' I frowned at her. 'I thought you wanted me to tell you.'

'I do.'

'Da said that if you looked at glass close up, it would look like everything it's made of, melted together. Sand, too. Sand would look like tiny shells.'

'How does he know?'

I flushed. 'He's just guessing. But it would make sense.'

I waited for her to mock me, but she only said, 'I'd like to see sand close up.'

We watched the fire churn, silent a while. Then Lupe asked, 'Does glass melt, then?'

I knew what she was really asking.

'I suppose it must, if it's made by melting.'

'Yes,' she said. 'Doesn't seem fair, does it? To be so close to the sea and not reach it.'

'A bit like being back in Gromera,' I said.

Her grin faded. 'I suppose.'

We watched the glass. Not long left now. Soon it would shatter, or melt, and there would be nothing between us and Yote's flames.

'What happened, then?' Lupe asked, in that way she had of picking up a conversation long dropped. 'Did you fall, or . . .'

'I don't know,' I said quietly. I was sure I had heard Yote, sure I had left my body, but it wasn't possible. It didn't matter now. Nothing mattered, nothing would matter ever again. 'I don't want to talk about it.'

Lupe took my hand. 'How about I tell you a story?'

'A story or a myth?' I asked slyly.

But she only put on a serious face and said, 'Definitely a story.'

'All right.'

She cleared her throat theatrically.

'Once there was a girl. This girl was a map-maker's daughter, but she insisted on everyone calling it cartography or something, and she thought her stories were the best and didn't want anyone else to tell them—'

I jabbed her hard in the side.

'That wasn't really the story!' she spluttered.

'I guessed.'

The glass made a grinding sound, and we jumped. There was no crack yet, but the shift and slide was more obvious now.

'Better hurry,' I said.

We sat cross-legged in front of each other. Lupe began again.

'Once there was a country where a kind king and queen reigned. One day, the queen decided to go on a tour of her lands. She set off alone on a horse, for she was a strong rider. But a couple of days later, the king received a message from the village she was expected at first. She had never arrived.

'The king rode for days, visiting village after village, enlisting more people to help him search for her. A week passed, and the king collapsed, exhausted. They could not find his wife.

'The loss turned the king mad. The trees stopped bearing fruit, and the rivers turned brown in their beds. The people wilted, grey as the sky. But this was not enough suffering for the king. He ordered higher taxes, and organized troops of soldiers to visit other nearby lands and bring back map-makers. He became obsessed with charting his country.

'Map-maker after map-maker came, but they were never good enough. The king wanted the maps to be bigger, more detailed. Then his men brought him a cartographer from the East, a clever, kind man, who realized how much pain the king was in and vowed to do his best to help him. The cartographer came up with an idea. He proposed making a map without a scale, or rather, a map to the exact scale of the land—'

'How do you know what a scale is?' I couldn't help myself.

Lupe regarded me wearily. 'I do listen, you know.'

As if on cue, the glass creaked. I spun around, but before I could look, Lupe grabbed my arms.

'It's better not to look. Trust me.'

I nodded, holding her gaze. She took my hand again, and continued, talking faster.

'The first things a map-maker needs are paper and ink, and to read the stars. While the cartographer made star charts, great nets were set out across the forest to catch each insect. They were crushed to make different colours, and soon the cartographer had a hundred vats of ink to use.

Then the forests were felled to clear the view of the sky. Tree after tree was mashed with gallons of river water to make the paper. All the animals died, and people began to be poisoned by the soiled river water, but the king did not care. He only wanted to find his wife.

'The cartographer began. He started at the western shore, laying down the paper and marking it with where the houses and roads and rivers were. When he covered the crops with paper, they died from lack of sun, but still the king did not care. His subjects began to leave the land and sailed to other countries, to be ruled by men less mad and cruel.

'Soon only the king and his cartographer remained. The map was almost done when the cartographer found the skeletons of the queen and her horse on a remote stretch of coast. He rode across the paper miles to tell the king.

'The king was so overcome with grief that his heart began to burst. The doctor had fled the place long ago, so there was nothing to be done. He died in the cartographer's arms.'

She stopped. I shuddered.

'What happened to the map?'

Lupe let out a bark of laughter. 'Only you would ask, "What happened to the map?".'

I waited. 'But what did?'

She shrugged. 'I don't know. The rain broke it to pieces, or the cartographer made it into a paper ship and sailed out to sea.'

'Really?'

'You know it's just a story?'

'Yes,' I paused. 'It was the best story I've ever heard. Who told you it?'

She grinned broadly. 'You did.'

'No, really.'

'You,' she repeated, softer this time.

My smile faded. 'What?'

'You made it up for my birthday. Three years ago, when we first became friends. You made me a map to the rabbit warren and we sat by it while you told me. I liked it so much I wrote it down when I got home. You really don't remember?'

I shook my head slowly. I only remembered realizing too late that I didn't have a present for Lupe, and telling her the first thing that came into my mind. I had no idea she liked it enough to memorize it, let alone write it down.

'I read it all the time at home. It has your favourite things. Adventure, maps . . .'

'And a sad ending,' I added.

'And that.'

The glass creaked, and this time Lupe was too slow to stop me looking. Near the top, where the glass was thickest, a crack had split the pane like a fissure in rock. A flame licked the centre of the line and the glass bubbled.

We broke away from each other, throwing ourselves backwards. The flames had not yet come through, but whole swathes of the surface were sliding down, bubbling into a threatening pool at the bottom.

I backed right up against the opposite wall of the glass-fronted cave. Something jabbed into my head.

'Ouch!' My fingers came away sticky with blood.

Lupe staunched the flow with her raggedy dress. 'What happened?'

'I hit my head.'

'What on?'

I snatched the wood-light from my belt and held it up to the wall.

Jutting from the surface was a shadowy shape. It looked like an irregular piece of rock, only lighter. But when I held the wood-light closer, it glinted.

It was not rock at all. It was metal.

CHAPTER
TWENTY~THREE

'It can't be . . .' I murmured. 'Arinta's sword?'

But it had to be. The shape was rusted with age but if I squinted I could change the indentations on its surface into engravings. And if it was, and if I was right about the sea being the other side of this rock . . .

Only the sea can defeat a fire demon.

This was our final chance, a gift passed down through a thousand years. I had said it myself, that glass was molten sand. That meant we were beneath a beach – maybe even the beach near Gromera. And that roaring, the roaring that sounded so much like wind and fire and, most of all, water . . .

I brushed my fingers against the sword. It was hot, the metal dull and unpolished, but I felt a surge of energy rush though my skin. My heart threw itself against my chest. I tried to grasp the hilt, but the metal was too hot. I bunched my tunic in my hand and tried again, but it was stuck fast. I wrenched and wrenched until Lupe placed a gentle hand on my shoulder.

The fight went out of me like air. I felt tears starting in my eyes, gritty and hot. 'You're right,' I said bitterly. 'I'm not her.'

'But the sword's here!' Lupe pulled me into a hug. 'It's real, Isa. It's not a story.'

I sniffed. I had been so sure the sword would turn for me.

Behind us, the glass gave another crack. An intense heat flooded the cave and I looked around in time to see the cracks open into a hole, small but filling rapidly with flame. The air seemed to suck itself through, draining the cavern and filling it with heat. As we watched, the glass dripped down, widening the crack, letting a thin stream of molten rock thread its way through.

I turned to Lupe, but she had already placed her hand on the hilt. I saw it blister and smelt burnt skin.

'Lupe, stop!' I tried to pull her scorched hand away but she pushed me back, eyes wild.

'I have to, Isa! I have to make amends—'

'For what?'

'My father.'

'I don't understand.' I reached out to her but she stepped back, shaking, blazing with anger.

'My father knew. He didn't believe it, but he knew about Yote.'

I gaped at her.

'The letter said so.' Lupe dug her fingernails into her palms and I could see the skin peeling. 'That's why he came here. He killed his father and was sent here as punishment.'

'For redemption,' I murmured, but Lupe had not heard me.

'He was meant to help everyone leave, help them escape Yote, but he took over instead. He was rotten, like you said.'

'It's not your fault,' I said carefully, trying to make sense of what she was saying. The Governor had known Yote wasn't a myth? But before I could ask more she gripped the hilt again. The metal fizzed against her palms.

'Lupe, don't!'

I started towards her but suddenly—

'It's working!'

The sword began to move, to turn.

A thousand years of pressure seemed to release in an instant, though this instant separated itself into distinct moments that would burn in my mind for ever.

First, another hiss rose to join the one from Lupe's palms. The second moment, a thin stream of water began to spurt out. The third moment, it grew into a torrent.

Just as the fire broke through the glass with a deafening crash, the water threw itself towards it. We collapsed under the weight of the sea.

Somehow, we found each other's hands.

The world turned, not only upside-down, but side to side. The ground was ripped again and again. I held on to Lupe in the tumult – or was it that she held on to me? –

though her fingers had to be painful from turning the sword. I was pressed down, ears popping as the force of the ocean pinned us in its grasp, thrusting us deeper.

We were drowning. Pressure roared through my head. My eyes bulged, breath forced from my chest.

The water smashed through Yote's thousand-year labyrinth as though it were paper, buffeting us along its relearnt currents, its power finally released. All I could do was hold fast to Lupe's hand. It was the only thing anchoring me.

As suddenly as the world had turned inside out, it righted.

My head surfaced, hitting solid rock. I spluttered, spitting out water and blood. My tongue throbbed where I'd bitten it. Lupe surfaced beside me. My arm was being pulled to the surface too and then I realized why: I was still holding the wood-light. It was bobbing on the rushing water, steadfast as Great-Great-Grandfather Riosse's boat.

I pulled Lupe forward, and she grasped the wood-light too. Gripping on to it and each other, we rode the steaming sea through what I could only guess was one of the tunnels that made up the maze. There was no sign of Tibicenas, nor of Yote or his flames. He was gone, swallowed by the ocean.

Our legs were being snatched at and wrenched down, even as the wood-light kept us afloat. I clenched my teeth as my feet were swirled and pulled until I felt sure my ankles would break.

We were swept into a high cave. My feet scraped

painfully along the submerged rock, caught between the current and the stone. I cried out, and felt Lupe kick my feet out of the way. There was a strange feeling of resistance, and a dull *thunk*, like a clay pot breaking. Then the current released us slightly.

I coughed up water. 'Are you all right?'

Lupe turned her exhausted gaze upon me, bringing up a lungful of water so violently she almost lost her grip on the wood-light. She was hurt.

'Hold on!' I clamped my hand over hers, looking around frantically. A few metres away, a fainter patch of dark caught my eye.

There was an opening.

I shouted for joy and instantly swallowed a mouthful of salty water.

'Look!'

Lupe's eyes lifted, and she nodded. But there was something wrong. Her pupils were huge, as if night had slid beneath them. I kicked her, my movements slowed by the sea, tried to keep her awake. She must have hit her head.

I brought my mouth close to her ear and shouted, 'It's all right. I'll get us home.'

The water was rising quickly, and we tilted our heads back to keep our mouths in the pocket of air. I wrapped my spare hand around Lupe's waist, and began to kick towards the opening.

The hole was perfectly round; it looked almost man-made. Objects were bobbing on the water – bits of cloth, and something that looked very much like bone. One nudged at my face and I pushed it away, fighting to swim closer to the light. It would all be worth it if I could only get us to the surface.

Just as the water started to close over our heads, I reached the mouth of the opening. I pulled Lupe beside me, and together we gulped in air. Above us the tunnel seemed to stretch for ever. Perhaps it would take us to a way out.

But it was narrowing. I could barely squeeze through. Suddenly, we stopped rising. My hand was wrenched upwards as the wood-light tried to stay with the surge.

I looked down, eyes stinging, trying to pull Lupe with me, but instead saw her dress tugging at her shoulders. It was caught on something. I tried to tear her free but her body was already wedged in the thinning gap. She was stuck.

We were running out of time. The water was high over our heads. My body convulsed, desperate for air. Lupe pushed at me. I saw her mouth working and shook my head. I couldn't tell what she was saying.

She tried again, smiling sadly, bubbles spiralling: *Still the smallest in the class . . .*

Then she tried to let go of the wood-light.

I clenched my hand around hers. *No.*

Time suspended itself like a stopped clock as we gazed at each other's blurred faces through the whirling water. My head felt full and empty at the same time, aching. The bright stars were back, my chest screaming.

Lupe squeezed my hand softly, and rammed the sharp point of the wood-light into my shoulder.

I gasped and rose, fast as a bubble, Lupe slipping through my fingers.

The pain of my shoulder wrapped itself around me. I tried to pull the wood-light out, but could not. I looked down through the reddening water, and saw that Lupe's arm was raised, the bracelet glinting on her wrist, her face calm, the last circles of air leaving her mouth.

Then she was gone.

CHAPTER
TWENTY~FOUR

The water spat me into more dark.

     I landed, hard, not on earth, but on rock. It forced the wood-light out of my shoulder, and agony rolled across my body. Blood spread warmly over my tunic as voices broke over me like a wave.

'It's a child!'

'What's happening?

'Where's the water coming from?'

I vomited seawater, skin stinging with salt. More water was rushing from the circular hole by my head. Many sets of hands were pulling me away.

I was lifted beneath my armpits, made to stand. I swayed, feeling water rushing over my ankles. Voices reverberated all around, and a horrid stench of mould and rot reached my nostrils. I knew this smell. I opened my eyes.

Uncomprehending faces stared back, blinking in the glow from the wood-light.

I was in the middle of the Dédalo.

'The underworld is emptying!' shrieked a man excitably.

'It's Isabella!' said another voice. My eyes darted around. That voice . . .

Pablo loomed over me, Masha at his side, more hunched than ever. How was he here? His face was stitched roughly at the forehead and chin, but he was smiling. The old woman unwrapped her shawl and tied it tightly around the bleeding wound in my shoulder.

'Are you all right, child? How did you—'

'Look!' said the excitable man, pointing down.

The water was still rising. The wood-light bobbed by my calves and I picked it up with my good hand. Everyone began running in the same direction. Pablo threw a kicking Masha over his shoulder, and grasped me.

'Come!'

It was too much, all of it. I tried to wrench my hand from his but then in the silvery light I saw a familiar face. The figure came limping up to me and hugged me so tightly I could barely breathe.

Da.

I held him with my good arm until I was sure he was really there. Until I was sure I was really there. There was so much I wanted to say, but my throat was closed tight. He released me and took the wood-light so he could hold my hand.

Together we followed the fleeing crowds. Da leant heavily on me, but he was moving more swiftly than I thought

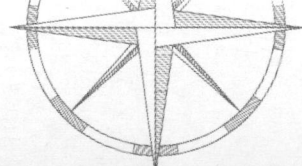

possible. The passages were nearly as narrow as the labyrinth. From the left and right came shouts of confusion, and more and more people flooded from the darkness to join the stampede upwards.

The water was sucking at my hips now, and I felt a fresh wave of panic as I looked up. A vast set of narrow stairs stretched before us, seething with people. From high above came cries for help, and hammering. We were not yet safe.

'What's happening?' shouted the woman in front.

The question went echoing upwards. A few seconds later, the answer was passed down the staircase.

'It's locked! The trapdoor is locked!'

Desperate shouts rose. The people behind were pushing forward, away from the swirling seawater, crushing us. Those already on the staircase clung white-knuckled to the thin rope that served as a banister. If the people behind kept pushing, others were going to be forced off the edge.

'Stop!' shouted Da, but it was no use. Panic had taken hold.

I racked my sluggish brain for a plan, but no ideas surfaced. The water was still rising, seeping into the bottom of my tunic now, my trousers soaked and heavy. I felt a sharp scratch through the material, and reached into the pocket to find the thin gold key poking through.

I pulled out the key ring. The six other keys glinted through the water. I tried to cry out, but still my voice would not come. I tugged at Da's sleeve and held them up. He looked blank a moment, then saw the royal-blue crest on the key ring. He shoved me forward.

'Go, Isabella. Run!'

So I did, every muscle in my body screaming to stop. I pushed blindly through the crowd, ignoring the shouts of anger and yelps of pain as I trod on feet and raked my nails across the hands that tried to stop me. The steps seemed never-ending, but just as my legs started to shake I saw the trapdoor, illuminated by a lamp swaying from a panicked man's arm. He was beating at the wood while another scratched at the lock, his nails bleeding, but no one came.

I pushed up the last few steps and pulled at the man's arm. He looked down, eyes wild, and I held up the ring of keys. He grabbed at them, but his hands were shaking so much he dropped them. They nearly fell off the step and into the crowd below. I snatched the keys up.

A scream came from the base of the stairs. I could not help myself; I looked. The water was up to people's waists. I shook my head to clear it, and reached up to test the first key, trying to ignore the tearing sensation in my shoulder.

It did not fit the lock.

I took up the next one, fingers trembling as the man beside me hissed fearfully, 'Quickly, child.'

More screaming was coming from below, and sounds of thrashing as the shorter prisoners fought to stay afloat, or were held up by their companions. The second key slotted into the lock but would not turn. Nor would the third.

Finally, with a deep wrenching sound, the fourth key began to turn. The man yelped in excitement and helped me rotate it in the rusty lock. Then he and two others placed their shoulders against the trapdoor and started to push with all their might.

They could not lift it.

One of the men screamed, pointing at the edges of the trapdoor. Huge, rusted spikes showed through. 'They've nailed us in!'

Then he was being pushed aside as Pablo moved past and put his shoulder to the wood. He heaved once, the stitches contorting his face, and the trapdoor swung off its hinges.

The light flooded over us like a wave, and the man behind me moaned, shielding his eyes.

Pablo jumped up into the corridor of the Governor's house, and helped me stumble out. I only had a moment to register that the torches were burning without a guard in sight, before Pablo grabbed me. He hugged me hard and I let him, gasping as my shoulder throbbed, his hands impossibly warm through my tunic.

Then he pushed me behind him against the wall, running forward to help the first rush of people scramble into the hallway.

A seemingly endless stream began dashing down the four corridors in an effort to make room, some joining Pablo in helping the elderly or injured out of the steep stairwell. The faces grew more and more harrowed, the clothes more and more soaked.

'Where's Da?' I croaked, as Pablo helped a woman out,

wet-haired.

Before I could stop him, Pablo was gone, pushing down the stairwell and into the sloshing darkness of the Dédalo.

I wanted to follow, but the throb in my shoulder had intensified and I stayed pressed against the wall. Opposite was the pinned butterfly and I kept my eyes trained on it as bodies rushed past. How could so many people have been in the Dédalo? An ancient-looking man emerged with a long beard wrapped around his arm, his eyes unseeing. Masha collapsed out of the hole after him.

Finally, I saw the top of Pablo's head, black hair flattened by damp, pulling someone's arm. Da emerged, dripping wet and sucking his cheeks in the way he did when he was in pain, and Pablo slung his arm across his shoulders to help him walk. It made me remember Lupe doing the same for me in the maze and I cried out as they hurried towards me. There were two more men behind them, and they seemed to be the last because together they heaved the trapdoor closed.

I was numb to everything except Da. I pulled away from the wall and forced my feet the few steps to him, falling into his arms.

An ear-splitting grinding spread through the house, a fierce tremor that ripped lamps from the walls. I tumbled to the floor, Pablo throwing himself over me and Da as the lamps smashed on to the cloth, spilling their fire.

We were helped to our feet and ran, all of us, down the corridors of the house like ants fleeing a nest. The flames were ripping at the ground, making quick work of the elegant tapestries and paintings. I felt like as if I was back in Yote's lair, and wondered whether we'd be crushed before we burnt.

The ground wrenched again, shaking the house. A huge crack opened in the wall of the corridor and my legs were quaking, skittering beneath me. But suddenly we were outside in the courtyard by the stables, and it was raining harder than I had ever seen it rain before.

The ground was churning mud, shaking so hard it was impossible to stand. I fell as there was another violent twist and a monstrous crunching sound that vibrated through my whole body.

A noise like thunder scraped the air. The stalls in the market square, pocket-small at this distance, were crumbling, sending up dust into the torrential rain. The Arintara was already bursting its banks to the north, flowing over the rubble, and the well in the centre of the square was sending water pluming upwards like a fountain.

'The sea,' shouted Da through a mouthful of mud. 'It's pulling Joya free!'

The sea seemed to give a last, brutal tug. The ground rocked from side to side, and I saw huge waves breaking over the bay below, sucking broken houses into the water. The blackened shell of the Governor's ship pitched and strained at its moorings, but I could see no other boats.

Wind whipped at our clothes, beginning to draw the rain clouds back like a curtain. They disappeared, the rain swept away with them, and we were suddenly dazzled by sunshine set against the usual blue.

The tremors slowed, then ceased. The ground stopped rocking, as if the island were finding some balance. I was winded, lungs useless as I tried to catch my breath. Around me, people were standing up, starting to call out to each other. Behind us, the Governor's house was shattered, the roof collapsed.

'It's floating,' said Da. 'Joya's floating. Isabella, what did you do?'

I could still not find my voice. The sea, the sea that Lupe had freed, had scooped out the base of Joya, snapping the island from its stem like a water lily. I had heard of floating islands, circling the world like living ships, at the mercy of the current. I had been entranced by those stories, but now I did not care.

As the blue of the Joya sky spread above me, and fathoms of sea flowed beneath, I closed my eyes, and wept.

Somewhere on the
WESTERN
SEA

One Year Later

CHAPTER
TWENTY~FIVE

Do you know how fast a floating island moves?
I do.

Some days it's like riding a giant sea turtle, slow as sleep. Other nights, when the moon is close and full, and the waves rise high as mountains, making Pep yowl, it's like running quick as the wind.

So the answer is: a floating island moves as fast as it wants to.

I think even Da thought we'd have reached some other land by now. According to his calculations, the current is taking us west. Towards Amrica. Da could board a passing ship and get there faster, but he says, 'Why leave a ship that is also our home? We'll get there one day soon.' Every day he charts our progress across the Western Sea on our walls. We've gone in so many circles it looks like Miss La's tracks.

She found her way home with Pablo, who regained consciousness after Lupe and I started walking the labyrinth. He called and called and was sure we were dead. When he reached Gromera, he told the Governor's men what had happened, tried to get them to go back and help, but they didn't believe him. They threw him in the Dédalo again, and it was only when the surviving Banished arrived that they realized he had been telling the truth.

That's when they nailed down the trapdoor, boarded whatever boats they could find and left for Afrik with Señora Adori. I am glad Lupe never has to know how easily her mother abandoned her.

Otherwise, less than you'd think has changed. My hair is a year longer, my shoulder nearly healed. My voice came back eventually, though I still don't like to use it much. Pablo's face has two thick scars across it, and I tease him that he's almost as lined as Masha. But really, I think he looks fine.

Da has built me a small room in the garden to work in. It's made of rushes and mud and we invited my class from school to paint it – only on the outside, though. Inside, I'm starting my own map wall.

With the port open again, we trade with passing ships, and most people have rebuilt their houses the same way. Da even bought some green paint for our new door, and a whole aviary of songbirds from a junk from Chine. We released them last week, and now they sing in every tree.

There's a tiny, jewel-blue one tweeting loudly outside, in Gabo's tabaiba bush. It's flowering again. The storm washed out a lot of the other plants, but this one only grows and grows. Buried beneath it are the Governor's keys.

I still don't honestly know what happened in the labyrinth. I told Da what I could, about the Tibicenas and the map's hidden layer, though he has only my word. The map is destroyed and the demon dogs vanished. Perhaps the sea swallowed them, as it swallowed their master.

It's hard to know the facts, or even if facts matter with an ending like a floating island. But I do know Lupe saved my life with her sacrifice. Saved all of us. Saved Joya, like Arinta did a thousand and one years ago.

There is no way I can say a true goodbye to her. But I can say thank you. I am finally about to finish my map of Joya, the island as it is now. Da and I have made three trips to see what I missed, and some of the villages are already populated again.

The forests are thick and green, and all the Gromerans got together to buy boar and deer from a ship from Europa. I saw a fawn on our last trip, drinking from the pool beneath Arintan. The waterfall is back to its full might, but I didn't go behind it to see where Lupe and I fell through. I don't like to be in a dark where stars don't shine.

Where the Governor's house used to be, a dragon tree has been planted. It grows higher each day, roots threading through the remains of the Dédalo.

I left this to last. The final landmark to be filled in. I

carefully stitch it into my map as a golden starburst, using the same spool as I did for Lupe's bracelet.

You're so sentimental, Lupe would say.

Next to it I write two words.

Lupe's Tree

I sit back, vision blurry from so many days crouched over the map. But when I blink down at it, rolling my sore shoulder as I trace the green of the forests, the blue of the rivers, the faint stitch of star lines – I don't just see ink and thread on paper. There's something else there – something close to the same life Da's maps have. Maybe.

Don't get big-headed on me, Lupe warns.

'Isabella! Breakfast's ready,' Da calls from the kitchen. The porridge smells as burnt as ever.

'Coming.'

I look down at the completed map, wondering whether to cry or laugh.

No point just standing there.

And I will not. With Joya pulled in the wake of an unknown current, I will never stand still again.

ACKNOWLEDGEMENTS

Every book is a team effort, and this one especially, so bear with me.

First thanks always to my family. To my parents, Andrea and Martyn, and my little brother John, for taking me on adventures around the world and around my head, for supporting and encouraging my writing, for being my friends, editors, proofreaders, cocktail-makers, travel-buddies, antagonists; whatever I needed at every stage. It all started with you believing I could.

To Yvonne and John, the least traditional grandparents in the world and therefore the best, for supporting whatever I've wanted to be however far-fetched, from first woman on Mars to poet.

To Sabine, for making me want to write stories you'll love.

To all the Hargraves and Millwoods and Karers and Kakkars and Slomans around the world who have given me books and stories and inspiration.

To Izzy, Hatty, Cecily, Ruth and Jess for your support, and for lending your various wonderful qualities (and in one case, name!) to my heroines.

This story is the last in a long line of drafts. Thank you to Amal Chaterjee, who set the assignment that started the story, and to Rebecca Abrams who gave me the tools to finish it.

To all my beta-readers who read multiple drafts: Andrea Millwood Hargrave, Tom de Freston, Janis Cauthery, Miranda de Freston, Madelaine Furnivall, Max Barton, Daisy Johnson, Sarvat Hasin, Joe Brady and Amy Waite. To Pablo de Orellana for checking my Spanish and helping me with pronunciation. To Tom Corbett for your kindness and belief. To the Unruly Writers – thank you for being cruel in your criticism and generous with your drink. Thank you to all the writers, reviewers and bloggers who have already been so supportive, especially Abi Elphinstone, Melinda Salisbury, Emma Carroll, Celia Rees, Lisa Heathfield, Lucy Saxon and Fiona Noble.

Sarvat and Daisy – one of the best parts of all this was writing with you two and becoming friends in the process. I'm so ~~jealous~~ proud of you both.

To my wonderful publishers on both sides of the pond. Melanie, your support has truly changed my life. Thank you to you and all the team at Knopf and Random House for your belief in the book. Victo Ngai, thank you for creating a cover that gives me butterflies every time I look at it. I hope to come visit again soon!

In Chicken House, the book has found a truly wonderful coop. Barry, Rachel L., Rachel H., Elinor, Jazz, Laura S. and Kesia: I have felt involved, supported and cared for every step of the way. Thank you. Rachel H. and Helen – thank you for a cover I have fallen completely in love with. Thanks to Daphne, copy-editor extraordinaire, and to Laura, for being a patient, thorough and supportive publishing manager. To fellow Chicken M. G. Leonard, for the encouragement and pep talks.

Thank you, Barry, for seeing potential in a confused manuscript, and thank you, Rachel L., for making it the book I always wanted it to be. Please always feel free to call on a Sunday evening to argue your case – you were right!

My agents: Hellie Ogden and Kirby Kim, and everyone at Janklow & Nesbit. Thank you for finding brilliant homes for my story. Hellie – thanks for having such confidence in me that I had no choice but to have confidence in myself.

Thank you reader, for choosing this book.

Last thanks always to Tom, my inspiration, my best friend, the reason I started writing and many other things besides. I hope you know this book is because of you – and your now patently disproved statement: 'You're too lazy to write a novel.'

'... a mesmerizing, enchanting debut, full of adventure and fire and heart. It reads like a fairy tale that's a thousand years old, so accomplished and rich and yet brand new and startling all at once. It's an absolute jewel of a book, as vivid and real as the maps inside it. It's a classic in the making and I know I'll be re-reading it again and again.'

MELINDA SALISBURY, *author of The Sin Eater's Daughter*

'Kiran Millwood Hargrave creates a spellbinding world of magic, myth and adventure. The story holds you like a labyrinth and won't let you go.'

EMMA CARROLL, *author of In Darkling Wood*

'A spellbinding adventure from a wonderful new voice in children's fiction. Beautiful storytelling.'

ABI ELPHINSTONE, *author of The Dreamsnatcher*

'A fine mix of magic and adventure with a captivating heroine – enthralling and engrossing by turns.'

CELIA REES, *author of Witch Child*

'... loved every second. Myth, magic, monsters, what more could you want?'

LUCY SAXON, *author of Take Back the Skies*

'Truly beautiful writing, within a magical world. I loved it!'

LISA HEATHFIELD, *author of Seed*

'Set in a vividly realized parallel world laced with magical realism, this is a mesmerizing debut of maps, myths and girls of enormous courage.'

FIONA NOBLE, *The Bookseller*